# FUGITIVE
# KIND

# BY TENNESSEE WILLIAMS

PLAYS

Baby Doll & Tiger Tail
Camino Real
Cat on a Hot Tin Roof
Clothes for a Summer Hotel
Dragon Country
The Glass Menagerie
A Lovely Sunday for Creve Coeur
Not About Nightingales
The Notebook of Trigorin
The Red Devil Battery Sign
Small Craft Warnings
Something Cloudy, Something Clear
Spring Storm
Stairs to the Roof
Stopped Rocking and Other Screen Plays
A Streetcar Named Desire
Sweet Bird of Youth

THE THEATRE OF TENNESSEE WILLIAMS, VOLUME I
*Battle of Angels, A Streetcar Named Desire, The Glass Menagerie*
THE THEATRE OF TENNESSEE WILLIAMS, VOLUME II
*The Eccentricities of a Nightingale, Summer and Smoke,*
*The Rose Tattoo, Camino Real*
THE THEATRE OF TENNESSEE WILLIAMS, VOLUME III
*Cat on a Hot Tin Roof, Orpheus Descending, Suddenly Last Summer*
THE THEATRE OF TENNESSEE WILLIAMS, VOLUME IV
*Sweet Bird of Youth, Period of Adjustment, The Night of the Iguana*
THE THEATRE OF TENNESSEE WILLIAMS, VOLUME V
*The Milk Train Doesn't Stop Here Anymore, Kingdom of Earth*
*(The Seven Descents of Myrtle), Small Craft Warnings, The Two-Character Play*
THE THEATRE OF TENNESSEE WILLIAMS, VOLUME VI
*27 Wagons Full of Cotton and Other Short Plays*
THE THEATRE OF TENNESSEE WILLIAMS, VOLUME VII
*In the Bar of a Tokyo Hotel and Other Plays*
THE THEATRE OF TENNESSEE WILLIAMS, VOLUME VIII
*Vieux Carré, A Lovely Sunday for Creve Coeur, Clothes for a Summer Hotel,*
*The Red Devil Battery Sign*

27 Wagons Full of Cotton and Other Plays
The Two-Character Play
Vieux Carré

POETRY

Androgyne, Mon Amour
In the Winter of Cities

PROSE

Collected Stories
Hard Candy and Other Stories
One Arm and Other Stories
The Roman Spring of Mrs. Stone
The Selected Letters of Tennessee Williams, Volume I
Where I Live: Selected Essays

FOR THE FIRST PRODUCTION OF THEIR TENTH SEASON

*The* MUMMERS

OF SAINT LOUIS

PRESENT

on

TUESDAY, NOV. 30
SATURDAY, DEC. 4

at

THE WEDNESDAY CLUB
AUDITORIUM

"FUGITIVE KIND"

By THOMAS LANIER WILLIAMS

Directed by Willard H. Holland

CAST

| | | | |
|---|---|---|---|
| TEXAS | *Frank Novotny* | TERRY | *Willard Holland* |
| JAKE | *Kenneth Sheehan* | REPORTER | *Ann Bono* |
| OLSEN | *Bernard Galvin* | GWENDLEBAUM | *Louis Prince* |
| PETE | *Victor Zuzenak* | LEO | *Samuel Halley, Jr.* |
| ROCKY | *Carl Koenig* | TRANSIENT | *Ralph Johanning* |
| GABE | *Carl Hohenberger* | O'CONNOR | *Albert Hohengarten* |
| ABEL | *Warren Hetzinger* | INTERNE | *Kenneth Kimball* |
| CHUCK | *Leland Brewer* | DRAKE | *Robert Baum* |
| GLORY | *Viola Perle* | BERTHA | *Mary Hohenberger* |
| MRS. FINCHWELL | *Erna Roth* | FEDERAL AGENT | *Fred Birkicht* |
| SYLVIA | *Lucile Williamson* | | |

Girls of the Junior Welfare League: Jane Garrett, Dorothy Timmerhoff,
Lucellea Mick, Jean Fischer.

Scene: The play takes place in a flop-house in a large middlewestern
city during the holiday season.

| | | | |
|---|---|---|---|
| Scene 1. | Xmas Eve | Scene 5. | December 30 |
| 2. | Xmas Day | 6. | New Year's Eve |
| 3. | December 28 | 7. | One Hour Later |
| 4. | December 29 | 8. | Five Hours Later |

(12-Minute Intermission After Scene 4.)

In "Fugitive Kind" The Mummers of Saint Louis present the second play by their
own playwright, Thomas Lanier Williams. "Fugitive Kind" justifies The Mummers'
conviction that Mr. Williams has an important contribution to make to the American stage
in the field of realistic drama.

THE MUMMERS OF SAINT LOUIS
BOARD OF DIRECTORS

Wesley Gore, Genevieve Albers, Robert Bennett, Fred Birkicht, Leland Brewer,
Jean Fischer, Sam Halley, Jr., Albert Hohengarten, Amber Gleave, Ruth Moon, Miriam
Schwarz, Dorothy Timmerhoff, Walter Geary, Mary Hohenberger, Viola Perle.

TICKETS FOR INDIVIDUAL PRODUCTIONS—$1.00, 75c and 50c

SEASON DISCOUNT BOOK CONTAINING FOUR $1.00 TICKETS—$2.00

For information on ticket reservations, season membership, associate membership, active
membership, classes for non-members, write: The Mummers of Saint Louis, 4477 Olive St.

THE MUMMERS BRING TO ST. LOUIS
THE OUTSTANDING NEW YORK SUCCESS
MAXWELL ANDERSON'S
COMEDY

"HIGH TOR"

DRAMA CRITICS' 1937 PRIZE PLAY
WATCH FOR PRODUCTION IN JANUARY

Cast list from an autographed playbill for the premiere
production of *Fugitive Kind*.

# TENNESSEE WILLIAMS

# FUGITIVE KIND

EDITED, WITH AN
INTRODUCTION, BY
ALLEAN HALE

A NEW DIRECTIONS BOOK

*Fugitive Kind* is published by arrangement with The University of the South, Sewanee, Tennessee.

Thanks are due to the Harry Ransom Humanities Research Center, University of Texas at Austin where the original typescript is housed. "The White Winter" and an excerpt from an unpublished poetic memoir of Clark Mills are from the collection of Remy McBurney (Mrs. Clark Mills McBurney).

Special thanks are due to Thomas Keith for his invaluable help in preparing the manuscript. Allean Hale is grateful to Albert J. Devlin and Nancy M. Tischler, editors of *The Selected Letters of Tennessee Williams,* for their generosity in sharing information and research; and to Margaret Thornton, editor of *The Journals of Tennessee Williams* for her important contributions from those sources.

Manufactured in the United States of America
New Directions Books are printed on acid-free paper.
First published as New Directions Paperbook 915 in 2001
Published simultaneously in Canada by Penguin Books Canada Limited
Book design by Sylvia Frezzolini Severance

Library of Congress Cataloging-in-Publication Data

Williams, Tennessee, 1911-1983.
    Fugitive kind / Tennessee Williams ; edited, with an introduction by Allean Hale.
       p. cm.
    Previously unpublished play written by Williams in 1937.
    ISBN 0-8112-1472-9 (acid-free paper)
       I. Hale, Allean, 1914- II. Title.

    PS3545.I5365 F84 2001
    812'.54—dc21

                    00-067321

New Directions books are published for James Laughlin
by New Directions Publishing Corporation,
80 Eighth Avenue, New York, NY 10011

# TABLE OF CONTENTS

# THE WHITE WINTER

All one winter the snow, soundlessly falling,
hushed the locked city, muted the powerful bells
and blurred at their source the stir and tumult of the thoroughfares.
For many days and many weeks
the snow fell without interruption through the windless air:
the great flakes drifted with a slow downward gravitation
over the northern river-bluffs, beyond St. Charles, and in the Plaza
    square,
The cathedrals were lost in a cloud that fell and froze;
the Missouri-Pacific, the Union Light and Power
went softly under;
shacks and stalled limousines were buried as the snow-flood rose.

Softly, softly
the hush, the unbroken hiss, the feathery thunder
rustled throughout the length and breadth of heaven.
East from an upper window I could see
the hanging streetlamps and the starred light
past which the snowflakes from the penumbra danced and
    sparkled,
bloomed three times and were gone.
                        Buoyant and white,
in city and county the snow fell night and day,
rose to the fencetops, levelled the icy furrows, erased the roads
and shored itself in drifts among the suburban farms.

This was a curious, hermetic season;
I walked and stood alone, with none but the city in my thoughts,
as the still city lay
under the trembling veil, the hush, the cold white hover;
in the suburban dark I stood, the enchanted lover
keeping one season's watch over the loved stranger sealed away,
chilled and oblivious with sleep.


All one winter about me, and about the city,
the silence and the fallen snow lay deep.

—Clark Mills

# INTRODUCTION

## A PLAYWRIGHT TO WATCH

*Fugitive Kind,* Tennessee Williams's second long play, written in 1937 when he was twenty-six, is full of surprises. It is a veritable index to his later work as he tries out characters, situations, and themes he will develop in plays from as early as *Battle of Angels* [1940] to as late as *The Red Devil Battery Sign [1975].* It is a surprise that, as an apprentice playwright, his source was the movies and more surprising to discover him as a radical writer. The Depression, which forced him to quit college to work in a shoe factory for three years, had politicized him. When Tom entered night school at Washington University, he was further politicized by his friendship with Clark Mills [McBurney]. Tom considered himself a poet at the time, and Clark was the outstanding college poet. Clark was also an editor of *The Anvil, The Magazine of Proletarian Fiction* published by Jack Conroy, a Marxist writer. Conroy's book, *The Disinherited* (published in1933 and praised by reviewers from *The New Republic* to *The New York Times* as the most representative work of the Depression) made him a hero to the young artists and writers on relief who met at the Old Courthouse on the riverfront. Tom joined them on Saturdays when he was off work. The book's homeless characters, and especially its title, may have been in Tom's memory when he wrote *Fugitive Kind.*

For once we know the origin of an undiscovered Williams play. In January, 1937, Tom wrote in his journal that he had seen a "lovely" motion picture, Maxwell Anderson's *Winterset.* "There were some shots of Brooklyn Bridge that were fairly breathtaking. I can well understand Hart Crane's inspiration by this . . . probably the most exciting piece of architecture in America." Jo Mielziner's set, the soaring expanse of Brooklyn Bridge receding into the fog, became more famous than the play itself. Inspired by the set and by his favorite poem, Hart Crane's "The Bridge," Tom laid his new play on the St. Louis waterfront near Eads Bridge, itself famous as the first steel bridge in the world. While the bridge is only mentioned in Williams' play as the place of Leo's attempted suicide, it becomes a metaphor for the play itself as a bridge to Williams's future works.

Tom was politicized further by The Mummers, an activist theatre group, who produced his first long play, *Candles to the Sun,* in March, 1937. A social tragedy based on a mine disaster, it drew extravagant praise in the *St. Louis Post-Dispatch,* citing Thomas Lanier Williams as "a writer of unusual promise." Willard Holland, the Mummers' director, urged Tom to write another play for their year-end production—which led to *Fugitive Kind.* Tom commenced it on June 5th in the attic of his parents' home, but the heat was unbearable and the clatter of his typing equally tiresome to his family below. More congenial was Clark's basement where the two set up their "literary factory." In a poetic memoir written several years later, Clark recalled "that dim cellar. . . .

> each of us on a kitchen chair, your typewriter
> fluent as automatic gunfire, as you sketched
> gestures and intonation, dialogue, behavior,
> and I with index finger, pecked and brooded,
> weighing the sound or color of a word.
> On one St. Louis summer day,
> sweat pouring down us, we conjured up
> —snow!
> Once, I recall, you thus explored a drama in a flophouse
> while I wrote of a winter white with tons of snow. . . . "

The merger of snow and flophouse became, for Tom, *Fugitive Kind*, and for Clark Mills a poem, "The White Winter" [p. ix] which would furnish images for Tom's play. So where much of *Winterset* takes place in the rain, *Fugitive Kind* would take place in the snow. From the first, Tom had trouble deciding on the direction of his play: would it be comedy, naturalistic slice-of-life, or lyrical tragedy? His fertile imagination could conceive the material in any genre, so he tried out various drafts before settling on a final version. Titles of drafts in the Williams archives at the Humanities Research Center in Austin show how his focus changed: *City of Dreadful Night* to *Clash by Night; Herman Never Loses* to *Cathedral Bells*. He finally compressed 543 pages into 104 for *Fugitive Kind*. His journal first mentions it on June 5: "After reading new play—laid in flophouse—felt thoroughly disgusted—will I ever produce another full length play that's worth producing?"

June 12: " . . . play goes badly."

June 30: "Wrote some good stuff—all but last scene of first draft finished."

July 4: "Saw Holland. . . . He read play, seemed fairly pleased though much rewriting is necessary. . . ."

July 6: " . . . the play smooths out but does not develop."

July 7: "I want to finish this new play—visit Memphis or the Ozarks. I will read the Pulitzer plays and then try to sleep."

Tom was aware that Anderson's stage play, *Winterset*, from which the film was made, had won the first Drama Critics' Circle Award; if only an apprentice, he was ambitious and sought out the best masters. He shared Anderson's indignation at social injustice, but he could not very well use Anderson's subject, the Sacco-Vanzetti case. (During America's "Red Scare" in 1920, two Italian-born radicals were unfairly convicted of a murder committed by a gang of bandits and put to death.) Nor could he copy Anderson's plot, a quest by one victim's son to hunt down the judge who falsely condemned his father. Without that play's core, Tom would feature gangsters. Tom may also have been influenced by seeing *The Petrified Forest*, which combined Marxist ideology with the excitement of American gunfights and introduced

Humphrey Bogart as the fugitive killer, Duke Mantee. As in this film, Tom has his characters trapped in a dramatic showdown. In *Fugitive Kind,* the lovers speak of John Dillinger, who was shot down on a Chicago street in 1934. They do not mention Bonnie and Clyde who died in a police shootout the same year, although Tom may have had them in mind as he conceived his plot. In St. Louis gangsters were not imaginary; Al Capone and his henchmen regularly visited a favorite bar across the river in East St. Louis when they needed to get out of Chicago. Tom's college friend, Jim Connor, who to Tom's disgust had become an agent for the F.B.I., became the G-man O'Connor, in his "flophouse play." (Tom's father called it the "G-Man play" which says something about the opposition between father and son. It would be one of the few works by his son that C.C. Williams admired.)

As in *Winterset* the main characters are a brother and sister with an elderly Jewish father. Tom's plot is simple. Terry Meighan, a gangster on the run from a bank robbery, takes refuge in the riverfront flophouse managed by Glory, Gwendlebaum's naive daughter. Sensing he is hungry and tired, she accepts him on trust. Now almost twenty and uneducated as shown by her speech, Glory has had to adopt a tough attitude through dealing with street people. Having had bad experiences with men, she has found safety in Herman, a boyfriend who does not even demand kisses. Terry, the mysterious stranger coming into her life is someone different—well-dressed, sophisticated. The play really takes off as he challenges her defenses: "Why don't you lay off the hard talk?" he says. "You ain't like that underneath . . . .You're lonesome like me." Terry fascinates her and becomes her catalyst for change. His "You don't belong here," underscores her urge to quit her dreary job. After he says, "You ought to wear bright colors," she appears in a red dress. Sexual tension builds between them until an accidental physical contact—as they touch shoulders to pick up some papers—leads to his rough embrace. He declares "You just found out you're alive." The underlying sexuality in their scenes is predictive of the new frankness Williams would bring to the American stage. When Terry saves Glory from a demented hobo's attack, he becomes her hero.

In Scene 5, Terry justifies his past in a long monologue, describing the circumstances that made him a gangster: his father killed in an accident when Terry was a baby, his tubercular mother forced into prostitution to keep them fed, his dead-end job in a slaughterhouse, finally his rebellion at never getting ahead, until he robbed a bank. Touched by his life-story of deprivation and convinced by his vows to "go straight" and to marry her if she will leave the country with him, Glory succumbs. Her sudden capitulation, as she forsakes the waiting Herman to run off with Terry—and her letting him take her to the hotel for three hours of sex before they leave—seems implausible, the more so since Terry has used her to open Gwendlebaum's safe to finance their getaway. At the end of Scene 6 Terry has a long poetic speech, the "aria" that will become a trademark of Williams's future plays. A polemic against the bosses who grind down the little "clock-punchers," it is more Tom speaking than Terry. Three years later, reliving his days in the shoe factory, he would write an entire play, *Stairs to the Roof,* on this theme. When Terry includes Glory in his declaration, "We're fugitives—but not from *justice. We never had* any justice!" it strikes a false note, as do Glory's ecstatic lines "You've got the cleanness of big things in you." However, Williams from the first had a strong dramatic sense, so that scenes which seem doubtful as read usually work very well on stage. Logic aside, the love scenes are the strongest in the play.

Lacking the plot complexity of *Winterset,* Tom introduced a group of characters who more than compensated. The brother-sister duo would be found in future Williams plays. The Jewish father also simply imitated Anderson's play: where Esdras is a rabbi, Mr. Gwendlebaum comes dangerously near to being a caricature, but is saved by a sympathetic portrayal. His dialect suggests that Tom may have intended to inject some humor into a too-serious script. He is the stereotypical Shylock, haggling over money, courting respectability, but as the play progresses, he becomes the emblem of the immigrant story in America when we learn how he adopted an orphan child on the ship to Ellis Island and named her "Glory" for the American flag.

Although Clark Mills said the play reminded him of Gorky's *The Lower Depths*, the strays who wander in and out of Tom's flophouse are his own creation. Their street speech, from railroad talk to drug jargon and jailyard slang, sounds remarkably authentic for a genteelly reared Southern boy. Their vivid characterizations predict what will be the playwright's greatest strength. Each has a history: the Swede Oleson, protecting his tubercular companion Carl, refugees from riding the rails; Jabe, the stool pigeon who connives to turn in Terry; Pete, who lusts after women; young Rocky, an initiate to the vagrant life; Abel a psychopathic fire-bug; and Chuck, who yearns to earn an honest dollar shoveling snow but can't afford to get his shovel out of hock. Bertha, the prostitute, is amazingly well-drawn by a writer who had never encountered her type except in imagination. The nearest Tom got to such an experience was when he and a friend ventured to East St. Louis to investigate the notorious red light district, but with no money to experiment, came on home. Knowing his father's reputation for "light ladies" doubtless roused Tom's interest; he would write a prostitute figure, variously called Bertha, Flora, or Bessie into several early one-acts: *The Dark Room, Hello From Bertha, A Perfect Analysis Given by a Parrot*, and would develop her character sympathetically as Goldie in *Not About Nightingales*.

Mrs. Finchwell and her Junior Welfare League illustrate Williams's ability to separate his actual self from self-as-observer. In real life, Tom enjoyed the attentions of the society girls he satirizes. He would note in his journal to which one's Country Club party he was invited, which was a maid at the Veiled Prophet's Ball. St. Louis society girls were among the group of "new women" who might appear at meetings of the Artists and Writers Union that met at the Old Courthouse; if they were slumming, they were also looking for something more exciting in life than parties. Tom had the same bystander view of his mother's upward climb in the D.A.R. He empathized with her efforts, but saw their ridiculous side. Mrs. Finchwell is the model for Cornelia in *Something Unspoken*. His dig at St. Louis socialites was the writer's revenge for how he and his sister, as newcomers to the city, had been excluded from the private schools which were the foundation of that society.

The most important of the minor characters is Texas, the wandering minstrel with a guitar who is obviously a sublimation of the playwright. He has been everywhere that Tom longed to go. If the other characters are sketched in, Texas is fully realized. He has the longest speeches and they serve to furnish exposition, comment on the action or move it forward. He is compassionate, showing sympathy to Abel when the others mock him, and to the dying Carl in his panic. Like Williams, he deplores the mechanistic world as a threat to the artist, and he expresses Tom's own despair at his no-exit situation. Of the major characters, two others speak for Williams. *Fugitive Kind* is a key to how Williams would create. He would consistently split one character—often based on himself or his sister—into two or even three opposites, or create characters from various sides of his own nature. From the first, as he confessed, his subject was his doomed family, from whom he seldom escaped. In *Fugitive Kind* he divides himself into three. If Texas is Williams the voyager, who would flee the workplace world through travel and his art, the boy Leo represents the early Tom, the collegiate rebel who ignored Journalism assignments to write what he pleased, the pacifist who skipped military drills and so lost his "scholarship," his father's financial help. Leo, a conscientious objector, has been distributing issues of the college *Clarion*, with his article on "Fascism and the R.O.T.C." Kicked out of school, he has tried routine jobs but is a dreamy misfit in the corporate world. Leo's lament, "The only thing I'm good for is putting words down on paper" is one of the most personal declarations in a Williams play. Terry, the gangster, expresses the violent interior emotions of the writer, whose journal records that he felt "like a coiled spring." Terry voices a theme which will recur constantly in Williams: that there is no guilt, that one is a victim of birth and circumstances beyond his control. This may seem a warped morality for one reared in a rectory by a grandfather who was an Episcopal priest, but in his first short play, *Beauty is the Word*, Tom had declared Art as his gospel. Nevertheless, he uses Christian symbolism in the names of the brother and sister: "Leo" the "Lion of God," represents the resurrection hoped for at play's end, which is further symbolized by the cathedral bells, the purifying snow, and the New Year. "Glory" is "Hallelujah!" These are early examples of Williams' fondness for symbols as shortcuts to meaning. Leo and Glory are joined in their longing for escape.

Williams's craftmanship shows him as experimental, a rule-breaker. The play is in eight scenes, rather than acts, which again is cinematic. Each has a commentary, a device he would use in *The Glass Menagerie*. Heedless of practicality, he creates some three dozen characters. Although the play's action starts as thirties kitchen-sink realism, its opening stage directions are expressionistic, calling for a large window which admits a skyline of the city, "as a great implacable force, pressing in upon the shabby room and crowding its fugitive inhabitants . . . against their last wall." The window, which frames the ever-falling snow with its suggestion of purity, the arc light beyond with its halo, the red light on the landing which illumines this little Hell and signals "danger" (this is where Terry will meet his fate); the cathedral chimes which build the tension of passing time, all these function symbolically. Williams introduces atmospheric music, which will become a favorite device, serving as a theme in *The Glass Menagerie* and a leitmotif in *A Streetcar Named Desire*. In Scene 7 the mood becomes frankly lyrical and Leo has his aria, an impassioned description of what's going on in a world at war while "God's asleep." "Justice doesn't come out of gun barrels," he says. In Scene 8 Terry is given a moving paeon to freedom just before he is captured. The finale is exciting, as lawmen and outlaw meet. Like

Val in *Orpheus Descending*, who will delay his escape to care for Lady and so be caught by the mob, Terry loses his life in pausing to care for Leo. This is perhaps the first example of a device Williams would use in *Summer and Smoke* and *A Streetcar Named Desire* where, at the highest moment of expectation, disaster intervenes. Leo ends the play with an argument Williams will give to Shannon in *The Night of The Iguana*, that if God seems asleep to personal miseries and world crises, humans will have to play God.

By September 16, Tom could write in his journal: "My play is almost finished." November 30 was fast approaching. Clark Mills had left to teach at Cornell University. The literary factory was closed and by October Tom was at the University of Iowa, deeply involved in one of the most intensive playwriting programs in the country. Meanwhile Holland had read *Fugitive Kind* to the Mummers and reported "God! What a reaction!" With the play in rehearsal and Tom rushed by assignments, revisions were carried out by mail. Holland and the cast seem to have done much of the revising. "We literally pasted *Fugitive* together," Holland recalled later. "We would read a page of dialogue . . . decide that two-thirds of it would play better in an earlier scene, scissor the stuff we liked and then paste it into a scrapbook. . . ."

Tom drove to St. Louis for the performance at the Wednesday Club auditorium on December 4th. He took one look at the set and was horrified. He had conceived the entire play around the big window which framed the falling snow. Now the window had changed to a transom at the top of the back wall. Years later he described his reaction: "I fled from the theatre and walked along the street literally tearing the script to little pieces . . . " This is likely a dramatization of how he felt rather than a statement of fact, for Jane Garrett Carter who was in the play, remembers it differently. "We were in the dressing room and suddenly Tom ran to the window and said, "Jane, I'm going to jump." I grabbed him and said, "Listen to me, Tom Williams, you'd have to go head first, because it's only one story down and you'll just break your leg."

After he saw the play, Tom wrote Willard a letter which he may not have sent. Admitting he had written the script too hastily, he complained about the scenery: "There was hardly any effort at atmospheric build-up in the setting for the latter half. The lighting was all wrong—there was no bare window to bring the city and the snow onto the stage—what became of the cathedral-like effect which we had agreed upon?" The newspaper reviews noted his capacity for observation, his "first-rate theatrical craftsmanship," called the play vital and absorbing, but said that "the last curtain finds him groping." Colvin McPherson of the *Saint Louis Post-Dispatch* said "the play describes vividly the life in a big city 'flophouse' but has no plot arising out of its situation. . . .With a wealth of colorful material in the characters who rent beds at 15 cents a night, Williams spends much time in merely loafing around . . . and listening." Reed Hynds of the *Star-Times* was kinder. He compared Williams to the current leading playwrights Sidney Howard, Ben Hecht and Maxwell Anderson, saying that Williams shared some of their faults as well as their virtues. "He wants to say something forceful and true about the chaos of modern life. But, like them, he seems clearer about the way to say it than what to say."

After graduation from Iowa in August and two weeks in Chicago fruitlessly hunting for a job, Tom had to return to an unwelcoming home. Here he must often have heard a variation of the question Mr. Gwendlebaum asks Leo: "Vot do you intend to do vit yourself? Moon around home writink papers?" With his father hoping he'd be drafted and his sister now in the state asylum, he escaped to New Orleans just before Christmas. En route he mailed four one-acts and two long plays to a Group Theatre contest in New York, under the name "Tennessee Williams." In New Orleans he immediately submitted *Fugitive Kind* to the Federal Theatre director, hoping for a local production. "They like it better than any submitted," he wrote his mother, "but are afraid the social message might be too strong for a southern city." It was sent on to the regional director in Florida, who turned it down. By

January Tom had finished rewriting his play and sent it to the Group Theatre even though the contest deadline had passed. On March 20, 1939, came word that he had won a $100 award for the short plays called *American Blues*. His fate, along with his name, changed as a result, for it brought him to Audrey Wood, a leading New York agent. Warning him that honesty was one of her virtues, she told him that *Fugitive Kind* was not ready for submission. "You are not a finished dramatist, although I do say I think you are highly promising." It must have been then that our typescript was laid in a blue paper folder of the Liebling-Wood Agency and marked "Only known copy of complete draft." However, she mailed *Fugitive Kind* along with his earlier *Candles to the Sun* and two long plays he had worked on at Iowa, *Spring Storm* and *Not About Nightingales* in an application for a Rockefeller grant.

Winning the thousand-dollar grant enabled him to study under John Gassner, who was so impressed by the first play Tom turned in that he took it to the Theatre Guild. They optioned it for a 1940 production. The play was *Battle of Angels*. In it Williams, who would never waste any bit he liked, had enlarged the character of Texas, his traveling musician, into Val with his guitar. Glory, older and tougher, but still vulnerable, became Myra. He discarded his gangster; by the forties the romanticized gangster of the films had been replaced by the alienated killer of *film noir*. He redrew his minor characters as the southern small-town mob. The play opened in Boston in 1940 and bombed. Rewritten, it reappeared in 1957 as *Orpheus Descending*, inspired a film, *The Fugitive Kind* in 1960, and in 1989 after its author was dead, was revived to international praise as *Orpheus Descending* with Vanessa Redgrave. Three other of Williams's apprentice plays, *Spring Storm, Stairs to the Roof,* and *Not About Nightingales* had productions in 1998-99 and the year 2000. Is it possible that *Fugitive Kind,* when published, will take on a new life? As Reed Hynds, the St. Louis critic, wrote in 1937: "Tennessee Williams is a playwright to watch."

—Allean Hale

# PRODUCTION NOTE

"In 'Fugitive Kind' The Mummers of Saint Louis present the second play by their own playwright, Thomas Lanier Williams. 'Fugitive Kind' justifies The Mummers' conviction that Mr. Williams has an important contribution to make to the American stage in the field of realistic drama."

So read the playbill for the premiere production of the play on November 30, 1937. The announcement of Maxwell Anderson's *High Tor* as a coming attraction placed the novice Williams in distinguished company. The Mummers trimmed Williams' proposed cast to 25 and introduced an intermission after Scene 4. Williams' original script calls for a cast of more than 30 and describes the scenes as follows:

The lobby of a flophouse in a large Middle Western city.

Scene 1. Christmas Eve. "A Big Group Picture, All Smiling."

Scene 2. Christmas Day. "This Town's a Jinx."

Scene 3. December 28. "You Ought to Wear Bright Colors."

Scene 4. December 29. "Beanstalk Country."

Scene 5. December 30. "Me, Terry Meighan, M.D.!"

Scene 6. New Year's Eve. "Snow."

Scene 7. Midnight. "The Big Celebration."

Scene 8. Three hours later. "They Won't Ever Catch Our Kind."

# CHARACTERS

In Order of Appearance

GLORY
TWO ITALIANS
TEXAS
CARL
OLSEN
PETE
ROCKY
CHUCK
TERRY MEIGHAN
JABE STALLCUP
ABEL WHITE
MRS. FINCHWELL
SYLVIA *and the other members of the Junior Welfare League*
PHOTOGRAPHER
POLICEMAN
MR. GWENDLEBAUM
A DRUNKEN BUM
LEO GWENDLEBAUM
A TRANSIENT
O'CONNOR, *a Federal Agent*
TWO HOSPITAL INTERNS
BERTHA, *a prostitute*
VARIOUS TRANSIENTS
HERMAN
DRAKE
SEVERAL LAW MEN
POLICE OFFICER

# FUGITIVE KIND

# SCENE ONE

## "A BIG GROUP PICTURE, ALL SMILING"

*Scene: The lobby of a flophouse in a large Middle Western city. Outside the door, an arc lamp projects a bright electronic bow, spotlighting the passing characters. A large glass window admits a skyline of the city whose towers are outlined at night by a faint electric glow, so that we are always conscious of the city as a great implacable force, pressing in upon the shabby room and crowding its fugitive inhabitants back against their last wall.*

*A stair is visible with a red bulb at the first landing. The desk or counter is stage right with an office door behind it. About the walls are benches and one or two chairs. An iron glows hotly. A checker-board is suspended by a string from the wall. There is a large calendar with a single sheet for each day—so that the date is plain to the audience. OKAY BEDS 15¢ is printed on window and on placard by desk.*

*When lighted the set is realistic. But during the final scenes of the play, where the mood is predominantly lyrical, the stage is darkened, the realistic details are lost—the great window, the red light on the landing and the shadow walls make an almost expressionistic background.*

*As the curtain rises a group of transients are discovered idling about the room. Two Italians seated on the bench are playing La Morra, an Italian game in which two individuals extend fingers or fists simultaneously shouting out numbers (in Italian), the winner being the one who names correctly the sum of digits projected. As they play, they become more excited, their voices rise to a piercing screech, and they huddle toward each other like fighting cocks. Suddenly the door of the office is opened and a strikingly dark, vital girl comes out—Glory, Gwendlebaum's adopted daughter. Her long bob is parted in the middle and the soft hair flies loosely about her face. In dealing with these men she has acquired a hard, shrewish manner—she glowers and swaggers as though constantly on the verge of battle. But off her guard she is graceful and*

3

*relaxed and has all the charm and softness that a girl should have. Her presence in this place is unexpected, incongruous. She knows it and so is mostly on the defensive.)*

GLORY [*fiercely*]: Victor!

ONE OF THE ITALIANS [*tone of nasal inquiry*]: Nanh?

GLORY: You two quit yellin' like that. There's men upstairs tryin' t' sleep.

VICTOR: Nanh.

[*They look at her sheepishly till she withdraws. Then begin playing again in whispers that rapidly rise to nearly the same pitch as before. A tall, gangling young man in clothes that are suggestive of the western plains slouches down the stairs. He carries a guitar and we know instinctively that he calls himself Texas or Slim and picks up loose change by use of his instrument and a thin pleasant tenor voice at cafes and beer parlors cheap enough to tolerate entertainment of this sort. He lounges on the end of the bench, strums and hums softly, watching the Italians' game. Glory bursts out again.*]

GLORY: I told you to quit that yellin'!

VICTOR: Nanh?

TEXAS: You heard the lady. Pipe down. [*He grins at Glory.*]

VICTOR: Nanh?

[*They stare viciously at Glory's back as she returns to office and burst into spluttering Italian with many gestures. Texas laughs and rolls a cigarette; he strikes a match in a cupped hand, ducking way over it as men do who are used to riding freight trains. During this business another group has entered the front door of the flophouse. Carl, Olsen, Pete and Rocky. The first two are old-timers. The other two are youths. Carl is coughing violently as he comes in. Texas looks up, then rises to greet Carl and Olsen effusively.]*

TEXAS: Well, I'm a green lizard if it ain't!

CARL: Hi, Texas.

OLSEN: Hiyuh.

*[They shake hands and arrange themselves about the room.]*

TEXAS: Where's the last time I seen you coupla kyowtes?

OLSEN: Huh?

CARL: Jungle outside Savannah. You was the guy that put that stinkin' rat's carcass in the slum. Had my belly tied up in knots for a week.

TEXAS: Rat's carcass your ass! That was a good shank of ham.

*[At this point Terry Meighan may enter unobtrusively and take his seat in the corner, unfolding a newspaper and holding it in front of his face. He is distinctly better dressed than the other men but unshaven. His nerves are raw from tension, hunger, lack of sleep. As he moves across the stage, he glances through window at the towering outline of the city and shrinks back from it to the darkest corner of room.*

*The outer door opens again and is held open for a minute by the new entrant, Jabe Stallcup, a small, cindery man with an air of desperate friendliness. The noise of the city crowds through the opened door, harsh, blatant noises and the cry of a newsboy.*]

JABE [*to Carl*]: Hello. Hello, Carl. [*Carl ignores him.*] You know me, dontcha?

CARL: Much as I want to.

[*Texas strikes a chord on his guitar. The Italians stop playing their game to watch.*]

PETE: Who's that?

CARL: A rat. Never got nothin' on me, but I don't like the smell of him.

OLSEN: No use gettin' him riled.

TEXAS: Jabe's a power with the local constabulary.

CARL: Hot in here like a furnace.

PETE: Feels chilly to me.

CARL: I'm runnin' a fever by Christ!

OLSEN: Naw you ain't runnin' no fever.

TEXAS: Bad cough you got there.

PETE: Last night he was spittin' up blood.

CARL: Yes, I commence to spittin' a little blood up last night. [*He looks eagerly, apprehensively about the room at all their faces as though expecting some startling reaction to this statement. Nobody shows much interest and so he relaxes.*] Not much though. [*To Texas:*] Ole thinks we oughta lay up till the cold snap's over.

OLSEN: Might as well rest for Christmas.

TEXAS: This ain't no weather for ridin' the blinds.

OLSEN: Naw it's naw weather.

CARL: Goin' Sout', if we coulda got to New Aw-*leens* before New Year's I figger I'd have a fifty-fifty chance of outlivin' another winter.

OLSEN: Quit talkin' that way. You're tough as you ever been, Carl.

CARL: Not too tough for them lab'atory rats to git their teeth in me.

TEXAS: What rats?

CARL: Lab'atory rats them amachur sawbones feed you to when you die in this town. Aintcha heard about them?

TEXAS: Naw.

OLSEN: One of his screwy ideas. [*His fingers describe cartwheels in air.*]

CARL: It's the God's truth I'm tellin' you boy! [*He coughs as though whole body would shake to pieces.*]

OLSEN: How you ben doin', Texas?

TEXAS [*looks serious, gives a 'bird'*]: All they want is a nickel's worth a canned music round here.

CARL [*examining shoe*]: What I tell you, Ole? Worn clean through.

TEXAS: Radios an' electric victrolas! —I pick up a few dimes now an' then.

CARL: God damn you, that rat's carcass tied my belly in knots.

TEXAS: I got that ham shank offen a Baptis' preacher's wife.

CARL: Ain't digested my food good since.

TEXAS: Summer before last, that calaboose in Mobile.

OLSEN: Huh?

TEXAS: That's where I seen you all last! They was bookin' you-all the mornin' that I got out.

OLSEN: Yeah.

CARL [*with sharp laugh*]: Suspected a rape!

TEXAS: You? [*He slaps his knee.*] Powder River—one mile wide an' two inches deep!

OLSEN: Funny you think, huh?

CARL: We nearly got strung. Strung a couple niggers on the same charge nex' day. Let us off.

TEXAS: Guilty?

CARL: Thanks for the compliment. You shoulda seen the bim.*

TEXAS: Yeah?

CARL: Had a corner on the beef-trust, that baby. Got hysterics. Ev'ry poor stiff they brung in, she says, Yeah, that's him, that's him! [*He spits disgustedly.*] Turns out later she hadn't been raped at all.

PETE: Some broad that didn't get her full price?

TEXAS: One nice thing about Alabama is they'll never hang a white man down there as long as there's a nigger left in the state. It's Gawjuh that I'm scared of. Them chain gangs, ever been on one a them?

PETE: Naw.

CARL: Naw, I don't believe in goin' t' hell till I die.

TEXAS: I have. I been on one. They put in a new kinda hospital treatment down there. When a guy gits sick they stick him in th' sweat-box.

PETE: I heard about them.

TEXAS: It's a sure cure for anything, boy. I seen a swell demonstration last summer.

PETE: Yeah?

TEXAS: A young punk about eighteen was doin a stretch for swipin' a flashlight. A nice kid but kinda sickly and that all-day

---

* Bim— A sexually loose woman.

work in the sun broke him down. He folds up an' the gang boss tells him he needs a little rest in the sweat-box.

PETE: God!

TEXAS: Yeah, they stick him in there an lock him up. Ever seen one a them things? It's a wooden box just big enough for a man to set down in. It's got an air hole in the top. That's all. They set it right out in the glare of the sun—and that Gawjuh sun is one thing that's got all hell skinned for heat.

PETE: You know it.

OLSEN: What become of the kid?

TEXAS: He cries like a sick dog all day. But toward night he quiets down. And when they come to stick his bread an' water through the hole in the lid they notices a kinda peculiar look on his face. His eyes wide open an' his face kinda purplish an' swole up. Didn't have a stitch a clothes on him.

PETE: No?

TEXAS: He'd torn 'em off like a lunatick does when he's hav'n' a fit.

CARL: Dead?

TEXAS: Kind of. God only knows how that bastard died. Suffocated or roasted to death. Or maybe just died of a panic. I did almost when they had me in it and Christ knows I'm not a sissy!

CARL: I guess they figured it saved the state some money.

TEXAS: No, suh, they'll never catch me alive again in Gawjuh, I don't care if it's just for liftin' a hen off a nigger's back fence. [*He rises and strums a lively tune on his guitar.*]

[*Glory enters and goes to the counter. Carl rises and goes toward her.*]

CARL: What's the price of a flop in this place?

GLORY [*pointing*]: Right there on the wall.

CARL: Fifteen cents? That's a helluva note.

GLORY: Pay now?

CARL: Wait'll I make up my mind. [*He returns to the bench.*]

[*One or two other transients pay and go upstairs to the dormitory. Glory takes some money from cash register and goes back into office.*]

PETE: Got a bim workin' here?

TEXAS: She's Gwendlebaum's adopted daughter.

PETE: Adopted? I wouldn't mind adopting a daughter like that.

TEXAS: He's opened up a new joint on Fourteenth Street so she's helping out over here.

PETE: Pretty good looker for a joint like this.

TEXAS: She's cagey as hell.

CARL: Fifteen cents. That's a helluva note.

PETE: Over at the Muny you can sleep for nutten.

TEXAS: Army cots.

PETE: You can sleep on 'em.

ROCKY: Let's go over there an save some money, huh, Pete?

PETE: How about it, Carl?

OLSEN: Hey, Carl an' me need a good sleep.

TEXAS: Over at the Muny you got to be fumigated first.

ROCKY: What's that?

CARL: Fumigated? [*He laughs and coughs.*]

TEXAS: That's classy langwidge for being deloused.

ROCKY: Painful?

PETE: Painful! [*He shoves Rocky's head.*]

CARL: Naw, it ain't painful but it's bad for a guy's self-respeck.

PETE: The hell with a guy's self-respeck when he can git a free flop.

ROCKY: That's what I say.

TEXAS: Over at the Muny you got to go through the showers.

CARL: Um-hm, I thought about that.

ROCKY: Water don't hurtcha.

TEXAS: Yeah, but they gives you a cold shower, buddy, and when I say cold I mean *so* cold that it makes a soprano out of a second bass. [*They laugh.*]

CARL: No, the Muny's no place for you punks.

ROCKY: Why ain't it?

CARL: They got guys over there can't sleep in their own beds at night.

ROCKY: Sleepwalkers?

PETE: Sleepwalkers! [*He shoves Rocky's head.*]

CARL [*laughing*]: You might call it that.

PETE: Don't try to explain to Rocky. Rocky's too young.

TEXAS: Powder River! [*He sings.*]

> I'm a rambler, I'm a gambler
> and I'm far from my home—
> If the people don't like me
> they can leave me alone!
> I eat when I'm hungry, I drink when I'm dry—
> If whiskey don't kill me I'll live till I die!*

[*He yodels loudly. Glory sticks her head out of office door.*]

GLORY: There's men upstairs trying to sleep!

TEXAS: Okay, Glory.

---

*"Powder River" was a poplular cowboy song in 1937. It has many variants. The Powder River is in Wyoming.

[*She goes back in.*]

PETE: Glory. Is that her name?

TEXAS: Glory Gwendlebaum. Some combination, huh?

PETE: Part of the accommodations, is she?

TEXAS: Naw, she's regular.

PETE: The bim don't exiss that ain't got her price.

TEXAS: That's what another guy thought. Went off his nut about her an stuck up a fillin' station so's he could make her a good proposition. Now he's in stir. And that's all he got for his trouble.

PETE: Them Jew girls are said to be pretty hot stuff.

TEXAS: She ain't Jewish.

PETE: Gwendlebaum's daughter?

TEXAS: Adopted, I toleja.

PETE: Oh, yeah.

TEXAS: Gwendlebaum's real kid is a boy name Leo. Writes poetry an' stuff. Goes to college.

PETE: Sissy, huh.

TEXAS: Better not let him catch you makin' a pass at Glory.

CARL: He'll learn if he keeps on livin'.

PETE: Aw, hell, what a life. Here it's the night before Chrismus. I ain't had a date wit' a bim since—

ROCKY: Since when?

PETE: Since that fireman's wife in Sioux City said she would sew up a hole in the sleeve of my shirt.

[*They laugh. Rocky turns and begins to laboriously print his name on the wall behind.*]

TEXAS: That's how it is on the road. It don't do to think about women. You're likely to go off your nut an' make a wrong pass.

PETE: Well, if a guy's good-lookin'—

ROCKY: Like you?

PETE [*shoving Rocky's head*]: No, like you!

TEXAS [*sorrowfully regarding his worn corduroys*]: Yeah, if he's got a good front.

PETE [*noticing Rocky's occupation*]: "A man's ambition is very small— Who writes his name on a flophouse wall!"

[*Chuck comes downstairs with a broom.*]

CHUCK: Say, do you fellers think it might snow?

PETE: What do you care if it snows?

CHUCK: If it did, I could pick up some money with my shovel.

CARL: First time I known you could pick up money wit' a shovel in this man's town.

TEXAS [*strumming*]: Ain't you heard? The Federal Reserve's got a surplus so they're sprinkling the streets with five-dollar gold pieces just to celebrate Christmas.

CHUCK: You guys think you're kiddin'. —They always want their walks cleaned off for Christmas out West End* when it snows. [*He moves over to the window and looks out.*]

CARL: Yea, so they won't fall down and bust their big fannies. Gimme some makins, Texas.

OLSEN: You oughten smoke wit' that cough.

CARL: Got nutten to lose, have I, Tex? Thanks.

CHUCK [*at the window*]: I got my shovel in hock. I could get it out for six bits.

CARL: Six bits?

CHUCK: Yeah, that includes intrush. I figgered it all up this morning.

OLSEN: How long you had it in hock?

CHUCK: How long? Since early las' summer.

PETE: Whatcha put it in hock for, screwball?

CHUCK: I got awfully thirsty las' summer. And winter seemed a long ways off. [*They laugh.*]

CARL: Winter's one bitch that *never* stands a guy up!

---

* West End—The play takes place in St. Louis where the West End is a fashionable district.

TEXAS: You can always count on winter.

CARL: Reminds me I gotta put some cardboard in these here boots.

TEXAS: Whyncha go over to the Sally* an git a new pair for nothin'?

CARL: First you gotta be saved. I ain't in the mood for salvation.

PETE: Wit' a cough like that you oughta be.

OLSEN: Carl's been coughin like that for years.

CARL: Yeah, I been coughin' like that for years. —Las' night I commence to spittin' a little blood.

OLSEN: You done that before.

PETE: Didja look to see what color it was?

CARL: What do you mean what color?

PETE: If it was bright red it means it comes from the art'ries.

OLSEN: Crap!

CARL: Naw, it was blue. Me being from the upper classes. [*He spits.*]

PETE: You oughta lay up in the free ward a while.

CARL: What? [*He rises tensely.*]

---

* Sally—The Salvation Army.

PETE: I said you oughta lay up in the free ward.

CARL: You're a pretty smart punk tellin' me what to do!

[*Abel White enters. He is a middle-aged transient of unbalanced mind. Years of lonely wandering have filled him with the desperate need to assert his personality to everyone he meets. His movements are slow and vague. He is a schizophrenic type. He first approaches Pete.*]

ABEL: My name is Abel White. [*He clears his throat and raises his voice.*] I was born in Sandusky, Ohio. Sandusky, Ohio! How old do you think I am? How old?

PETE: I woulden know. [*He moves to another bench.*]

ABEL [*loudly*]: I'm forty-seven years old. Next April I'll be forty-eight!

CARL [*still examining his shoes*]: I sure do wish I could git me a new pair o' shoes this winter.

TEXAS: Let Olsen take the nose-dive for you.

CARL: The Swede's pretty good at that.

OLSEN: Sure. I'll take the nose-dive.

CARL: Tell 'em how you seen the light in Mother Dempsey's parlor that time.

TEXAS: Canal Street?

CARL: Yeah.

TEXAS: I been there.

CARL: Y'know the Swede pours his religion out of a bottle. Beat any sky-rider on half a pint.

OLSEN [*seriously*]: I started out to be a preacher.

TEXAS: What stopped you, Ole?

OLSEN: Too much I coulden figger out.

TEXAS: You don't believe in God no more?

OLSEN: Oh, I take spells of believin' and spells of disbelievin'.

CARL [*grimly*]: When you're dead you're dead. The same as any cow is. [*He leans his face on his hands.*]

PETE [*to Rocky*]: Aw hell, gimme that pencil.

TEXAS [*grinning*]: Me I count on gittin' my reward in heaven all right! [*He strums.*]

ABEL [*approaching Carl*]: My name's Abel White. [*Silence.*] I come from Sandusky, Ohio. [*He fumbles in his pocket for a match, strikes it and watches it burn.*]

ROCKY: What's he goin' aroun introducing himself to ev'ryone for?

PETE: Screwball.

ABEL: Look at me. I'm alive. I'm human, ain't I?

CARL: Yeah.

ABEL [*striking another match*]: I was born in Sandusky, Ohio. Look how it burns. It looks pretty burning. I like to see things that color. I saw a girl once with hair the color that is. It caught on fire once. Caught fire and I watched it burning. Somebody said that it was my fault that it caught on fire and they wanted to kill me for it but I got away. —Why don't you say something?

ROCKY [*to Pete*]: I bet he did set it on fire himself.

PETE: The screwball's lyin'.

OLSEN: What do you want me to say to you, Abel?

ABEL: Anything. I get tired of not talking to people and people not talking to me. [*To Rocky*:] Have you got a match, boy?

ROCKY: Naw.

ABEL: I have three in my pocket but I want to save them. Sometimes I run out of matches. —Did I tell you about the time I saw a girl's hair catch on fire?

PETE: Naw. And you forgot to mention about the time that you was dropped on your head when you was a baby.

TEXAS: Go on and tell us.

ABEL: Lots of people start laughing at me that way. I think it's because I've got something wrong with me. [*He anxiously fingers his face as though suspecting some visible deformity.*]

TEXAS: Don't mind them.

ABEL: I'd like to have six more matches.

TEXAS: Here. [*He gives him some.*]

CARL: You want him to burn the place down?

TEXAS: Now go on and tell us about the time the girl's hair caught on fire.

ABEL [*striking a match*]: She had yellow hair like this. I wanted to stay and watch how it burned but she started screaming and some men came along and—they wanted to kill me. [*He strikes another match.*]

ROCKY: He set it on fire himself.

PETE: He's dreamin'.

ABEL: Now I've only got five left. But that's two more than I had before you gave me six. Look. [*He counts the matches on the bench. Pete and Rocky laugh. Abel slowly feels his face.*]

TEXAS: Don't mind them punks.

ABEL: You tell me something.

TEXAS: Tell you what?

ABEL: Anything. I have a sister that's living. But I haven't seen her in a long while.

PETE: Some hustler, I bet!

TEXAS: Shut up. I got a sister, too. [*He pulls out his wallet.*] Here's her pitcher.

ABEL: Yellow hair?

TEXAS: Yeah. She's blond. Her name's Alice.

ABEL: Let me hold it a minute. [*He takes the picture and gazes at it yearningly.*] I'd like to keep this picture with me.

TEXAS: Give it back.

ABEL: No. [*He crouches and holds the picture between his knees.*]

TEXAS [*wrestling for the picture*]: God damn you, you torn it! [*He twists Abel's wrist, forcing him to let go. He tries to smooth out the crumpled picture.*]

[*Glory comes out of the office.*]

GLORY [*sharply*]: I smell something burning.

PETE: This here screwball's been striking matches.

GLORY [*to Abel*]: Get out!

[*Abel rises slowly.*]

TEXAS: Go on, roll your hoop out of here! —He spoiled my sister's pitcher.

[*Abel shuffles slowly to door. He strikes a match on the side of it as he goes out. He can be seen through window creeping down the walk with his face bent over the match cupped in his hands.*]

GLORY: A firebug. I ought to report him to the police.

PETE: What makes 'em like that about fire?

TEXAS: I met one of 'em in stir once. He said that watching things burn made him think about women. It was just the same feeling that you or me would get climbing into bed with—

GLORY [*sharply*]: That kind of talk belongs upstairs.

TEXAS: 'Scuse me, Glory.

CARL [*reading paper*]: I see where the Mayor's fixin' to give us another one of his annual Christmas dinners.

TEXAS [*yawning*]: Big-hearted, ain't he?

CARL: The only big thing about that guy is the thing that he sits on. —Also says here that the Junior Welfare League will distribute baskets among the deserving poor.

PETE: Baskets a what?

TEXAS: Whatever they think the poor is deserving of.

CARL: Rat poison.

TEXAS: What's on the Mayor's bill a fare?

CARL: Lamb stew an' potatoes an' peas an'—

TEXAS: Sounds like plain old slum.

CARL: Coffee'n'canned peaches.

TEXAS: Yeah, same as las' year excep' they had cel'ry.

PETE: What's cel'ry good for?

TEXAS: Makin' noise.

PETE: Reckon there'll be a big crowd?

TEXAS: Ever known a bum to turn down a free meal? Neither did I. You're lucky to get your nose in the place.

CARL [*rising slowly*]: Well, the way that I'm feeling now I won't be living this time tomorrow. *(He pauses and looks out the window.]* The body awaits identification at the city morgue! [*He coughs.*]

GLORY: Are you feeling sick?

CARL: No. I just got a slight case of galloping consumption.

GLORY: You feel that bad you'd better go over to the city hospital.

CARL [*angrily*]: I'm payin' you for a bed, not advice.

GLORY: All right, Mister. [*He gives her fifteen cents.*]

CARL: All right. [*He goes toward the stairs.*] You think I want them white coated devils feeding me to their pet rats? Not as long as I've got two legs to stand on.

[*Noise of cars drawing up.*]

PETE [*at the window*]: Lookit them classy cars stoppin' out there.

ROCKY: Limoosines!

PETE: Yeah. Sassiety bims!

TEXAS: Must be that there Junior Welfare League.

[*A bevy of dazzling socialites on a charitable mission enter. Most of them are dressed for the evening. They carry baskets containing gifts. They are led by an imposing dowager with pince-nez and a chiffon handkerchief which she holds to her nostrils frequently. Most of the action will be ad-libbed, the voices a confused babble. A certain amount of burlesque is allowable but should not be carried too far. Our aim is to give a satirical, impressionistic interpretation rather than one of exact realism. It is the sort of overemphasis or humorous exaggeration that might be used, more freely, in a comic Russian Ballet.*]

MRS. J. MORTIMER FINCHWELL IV [*marshaling her flock*]: Now, girls, remember what I told you. These are bachelor apartments and we must remain downstairs!

[*The girls move animatedly about the room.*]

MRS. FINCHWELL [*to Glory*]: Oh, good evening. We're distributing a few little gifts from the Junior Welfare League as a part of our Christmas Activity program and we—Girls! Please stay away from the stairs! —Are you employed here? Really? These poor homeless men, etc.—

GLORY [*nervously*]: If you'll let me take the baskets, I could give them out in the morning.

MRS. FINCHWELL: Oh, no. Thanks so much, but we want to do it ourselves. You see the reporters will arrive any minute and—

GLORY: What reporters?

MRS. FINCHWELL: Photographers, too! —Girls! I suggest that we wait till the photographers arrive before we begin the distribution of gifts! I believe we have the gifts labeled, have we not, girls? And if any gentleman has a particular preference—say for shaving talcum, razor blades, soap, handkerchiefs, neckties!—I think it would be nice if you would come up individually and state your preference so that each and everyone will get exactly what he wants—don't you think that's a good idea?—and there won't be any disappointments!— [*She laughs with marvelous gaiety.*] Girls! I think we should wait till the photographers arrive!

[*The girls go among the men questioning them about desired articles. There is a confused mumble of voices. The men stare sympathetically or lustfully at the girls and are mostly resentful of their questions*]

SYLVIA [*approaching Terry who keeps apart*]: What do you want, Mr. Serious?

TERRY: Leave me out of this. I don't want nothing.

SYLVIA [*who finds him attractively different*]: Oh, but you must want something!

[*She shows him various things, trying to engage his attention. He is increasingly nervous. He rises and edges toward the stairs. The photographer arrives. There is an excited babble of voices.*]

MRS. FINCHWELL [*stridently*]: Girls! Girls!

PHOTOGRAPHER: All right, ladies, a big group picture, all smiling!

VOICES: Azalea Lofton de Smott Kensington—324 Royal Drive—lahst summer on the Riveria—the Ile de France—Bryn

Mawr—Vassar—Mme. Renaud's in Geneva—Mt. Holyoke—traveled abroad last summer in Mrs. Atcheson's pahty—Azalea Lofton de—Dorothy Stuart—Caldwell—Mrs. J. Mortimer Finchwell the Fourth—firm of Roger & Rogers—executive—Board of—girls, girls, girls!

PHOTOGRAPHER: Now, Mrs. Finchwell!

MRS. FINCHWELL: Oh, no, not me! Well—

[*Individual pictures are taken. Sylvia grabs Terry's arm forcing him downstage. He tries to break away, but she clings tighter, laughing shrilly.*]

SYLVIA: We want ours taken together!

TERRY: I don't want no picture. Leggo!

[*He shoves her roughly. She screams. Pandemonium. An officer steps in. Terry has gone to the foot of the stairs.*]

SYLVIA [*pointing to Terry*]: That man struck me! I want him arrested! Arrest that man!

MRS. FINCHWELL: Some of these men have really behaved very rudely. This one is a drunk and that one over there made an offensive remark to one of the girls. If we had known—

[*Gwendlebaum has rushed downstairs. He is the middle-aged Jewish proprietor of the flophouse.*]

GWENDLEBAUM [*frenziedly*]: Officer! Wrecking my place!

SYLVIA: I demand that you place that man—

MRS. FINCHWELL: Girls—outside—immediately!

SYLVIA: My father is Atherton Pembroke, President of the—

GLORY [to the officer]: He didn't hit her at all. She was bothering him and he tried to get away from her—

SYLVIA: What colossal nerve! You cheap little—!

MRS. FINCHWELL [at the door]: Sylvia! —The Junior Welfare League will see that the proper action is taken!

[With this ominous warning, Mrs. Finchwell conducts Sylvia—sobbing—outside. The officer recovers his poise and begins to bluster.]

OFFICER: Who started this fracas?

CARL: Them sassiety broads.

[The men mutter resentfully among themselves, still snatching and tearing at the packages most of which contain apparently useless articles.]

OFFICER [quieting them]: I got a notion to run you all in.

GWENDLEBAUM: Lookit my place here! A shambles! [To Chuck.] Clean up diss mess!

OFFICER: —If it wasn't Chrismus I would!

[Glory placates him and he goes outside where the girls are still excitedly gesticulating with another officer.]

GWENDLEBAUM: Papers an' ribbons all offer! Vot kind of girls vass dey?

CHUCK: Sassiety girls. A league of some sort.

GWENDLEBAUM: *Mein Gott,* da bush-leaguers! Deir papas could close da place op! [*Glory comes in from the street.*] Glory, vhy could you not prevent a ting like diss from taking place? I leave you in charge for a vhile and look vot happens! A regular shambles vit papers and ribbons and policemans and—Git on upstairs vit you men before you're locked up by da cops! [*He starts outside.*]

GLORY: Here's your overcoat, Papa. You better square things with the Captain. Your hat, Papa!

[*The men shuffle upstairs with their gifts, some angrily grumbling, some laughing.*]

GLORY: It's late. You'd all better go up.

CHUCK [*to Terry in admiration*]: Didja really take a sock at her?

GLORY: Go on up stairs, Chuck. I'll finish cleaning.

CHUCK [*at the window.*]: A'right. They're drivin' off now in their limoosines. [*Pause. To Glory:*] You think there's a chance it might snow?

GLORY: I'd like to say anything's likely.

[*Chuck goes up stairs. Glory leans against the counter, exhausted. Terry comes slowly from the corner; he straightens his collar, brushes his sleeve.*]

TERRY: I guess I'm a social success.

GLORY: Are you going to stay here tonight?

29

TERRY: After what's happened maybe I better clear out.

GLORY: Don't worry. Mike said just to forget it.

TERRY [*pause*]: All right.

GLORY: Bed's fifteen cents.

TERRY: I know. [*He approaches the counter.*] I'll pay for a week in advance.

GLORY [*smiling*]: Okay. There ain't any law against that.

TERRY [*suspiciously*]: What do you mean?

GLORY: Why, I just meant it's perfectly legal, that all. —What did you think I meant?

TERRY: I dunno. I'm kinda woozy tonight. [*He leans weakly against the counter and rubs his forehead.*] I need to catch up on my sleep.

GLORY: Been on the road?

TERRY: Yes. That's it. I been on the road.

GLORY: Oh. —You say you wanta pay for a week in advance?

TERRY: Yes.

GLORY: Let's see. Seven time seven is thirty-five and—that makes a dollar five cents. [*Terry rubs his head and seems not to hear.*] I said a dollar five cents.

TERRY: Yeah, I heard you. [*He slowly produces a bill, glancing at her cautiously as he does so.*]

GLORY: What's that?

TERRY: A bill.

GLORY: It ain't the usual color, is it?

TERRY: No, it's a century . . .

GLORY: You mean it's a hundred dollars?*

TERRY: Yeah.

GLORY [*after a slight pause*]: We don't see many of them around here.

TERRY: No. I guess you don't. It's all I got on me right now.

GLORY: I guess I'll have to get Papa to change it for you when he comes back.

TERRY [*after a pause*]: Will you? —No. Never mind. [*He sways drunkenly from weakness.*]

GLORY: Got something smaller?

TERRY: No, that's all I got.

GLORY [*noticing his weakness*]: What's the matter?

TERRY: Nothing. Forget it. [*He moves unsteadily toward the door.*]

GLORY: Where you going?

---

* The hundred dollar bill with the back printed in a yellowish color was called a "century" or "yellow-back."

TERRY: Out.

GLORY: You don't need to. [*He turns.*] I've took a chance on lots of guys that looked worse than you. There's no big rush about cracking that bill.

TERRY: No?

GLORY: Your credit's good for a while. You've got clean finger-nails and that's one thing that always puts a guy in favor with me. [*She rings the cash-register.*] Here.

TERRY: What's that?

GLORY: Some change. You better go round the corner and get some food in you.

TERRY: What makes you think I'm hungry?

GLORY: Your legs are about to fold up.

TERRY: I ain't had a bite to eat since day before yesterday morning.

GLORY: There's a quick order joint around the corner. Take this four bits and get you some ham'n'eggs. —You better let them centuries cool for a while.

TERRY: That's good advice, sister. [*Pause.*] How do I know you ain't gonna call the coppers and tell 'em you've got a suspicious character on the place?

GLORY: Yes, and how do I know you ain't gonna stick the place up?

[*Terry slowly removes a revolver and puts it on counter.*]

TERRY: Keep this for me.

GLORY: All right.

TERRY: I got no reason to trust you—except that you look on the level and you helped me out just now with them horsed-up floozies.

GLORY: Never mind about that. I seen you was tired and hungry, that's all, and I felt kinda sorry for you. Don't think there was nothing personal about it.

TERRY: No, nothing personal. [*He leans toward her.*] I was just hungry, that's all—hungry as hell! [*He tries to kiss her.*]

GLORY [*breaking away*]: Stop it!

TERRY [*breathing heavily*]: All right. [*Pause.*] You want your fifty cents back?

[*There is another long pause in which they stare at each other.*]
GLORY: No. Keep it. [*She goes behind counter.*] Just so you understand I'm not handing out nothing else.

TERRY [*with a grin*]: Sure, I understand. [*He moves toward the door, pulling hat down.*] See you later.

[*He goes out, looking furtively up and down street, and then moves past the window. Glory watches him from the counter. Then she goes to the window and stands looking out. Across the street the bells of a cathedral begin chiming the hour.*]

CURTAIN

# SCENE TWO

## "THIS TOWN'S A JINX"

*Early the next morning. It is dull outside: a fog has rolled up from the river a few blocks east. Figures pass dimly across the big window, shoulders hunched against the damp cold, heads bent low. The Christmas bells and streamers about the cracked plaster walls are totally unconvincing—life here is more like a perpetual Ash Wednesday than any other holy day of the year.*

*Chuck is sweeping away some of the last night's debris—tissue paper, ribbons, empty little boxes. His sweeping is farcical—like the movements of a deep sea diver.*

*A drunken bum enters.*

BUM: Merry—hic— Christmas!

CHUCK: Yeah? What do you want?

BUM: Look. 'Shall foggy outshide. People bump into me, don't even shay beg a pardon— [*He laughs.*] —I wanta resht here for a while till I get my directionsh back, huh?

CHUCK: Gwan roll yuh hoop outa here! [*He assists him out the door.*]

[*Leo enters during this episode, a slender, sensitive-looking youth about twenty-one.*]

LEO: Courtesy of OKAY BEDS! Come again, Partner, the house of Gwendlebaum is known from coast to coast for its warm hospitality, its cordial welcome to gentlemen of the nomadic disposition, the fugitive kind! [*He laughs and clumps a great package of papers down on the desk.*] Is that any way to treat customers?

CHUCK: That wasn't no customer.

34

LEO: No? He sure smelled like one. —Our exclusive clientele is invariably recognizable by their particular brand of polecat perfume, a subtle and exotic blend of— Hey! What happened here last night?

CHUCK: Nothing. We just had a small riot, that's all.

LEO: Yeah?

CHUCK: Da Bush-Leaguers paid us a visit. Santie Claus stuff. Distributin' bottles of lavender toilet water an' bon-bons an' little lace doilies—some of the boys didn't like what they got in their stockings.

LEO: Yeah? [*He is unwrapping the package which contains copies of a college publication.*]

CHUCK: Dey got excited an' honest to God the place was nearly blown up!

[*Terry comes downstairs quickly.*]

CHUCK: Ask him—he'll tell you!

TERRY [*suspiciously*]: What?

CHUCK: He took a sock at one of them society bims—didn't you, kid? Cause he didn't want his pitcher took for the papers!

LEO [*laughing*]: It's a wonder you're still at large!

CHUCK: Glory got him out of it. She soft-soaped the Sergeant an' he finally says jus' go back to bed an' forget all about it. —It's Chrissmus! [*He laughs.*]

TERRY [*snatching up the newspaper*]: Don't you think sometimes you make too much noise with your mouth?

CHUCK: —Huh?

[*Terry glances nervously out the window—a cop is passing—he turns quickly and goes back upstairs.*]

CHUCK [*slowly and emphatically*]: He don't belong here.

LEO: Obviously not. He's a pretty nice looking fellow.

CHUCK: Too nice looking. That's how I know. He don't belong here an' it don't take a gypsy to tell that he's gonna make trouble. I bet you we'll have to invest in a bran' new window before he's gone.

LEO: How do you mean?

CHUCK: That glass ain't bullet-proof an' when a fellow like him ducks for cover whenever a cop goes by, y'know things are gonna be popping around a place where he stays.

LEO: Big time crooks never stop at flophouses, yuh dope.

CHUCK: Naw. You wouldn't look for 'em here. Which might be a kind of advantage. —Where's Glory this mornin'?

LEO: Papa told her to take the day off—I'm gonna stay down.

CHUCK: He oughten to keep that girl down here so much. It ain't a good place for her. —Whoever heard of a girl workin' in a flophouse?

LEO [*laughs*]: Well, Papa's got his hands full over at the place on Fourteenth Street now, an' he says that Glory's the only one he can trust—you know how he is.

CHUCK: He could trust me.

LEO: Yeah? Our cash receipts would probably keep that hop-head girl friend of yours in a blizzard of snow.

CHUCK: Bertha? I don't truck with her.

[*Mr. Gwendlebaum comes quickly downstairs.*]

CHUCK: Mr. Gwendlebaum, don't I get time an' a ha'f workin' Chrismuss? Don't I get—

GWENDLEBAUM [*dashing to phone*]: You'll get time an' a ha'f on the seat of your britches! Operator, operator!

CHUCK: But, Mr. Gwendlebaum—

GWENDLEBAUM: Hosh op! Operator? Git me duh city hospital, I ain't got a number book wit' me! Yas. —Hospital? Diss is OKAY BEDS speaking, Sixth and Lafayette Streets. Ve got a case a something here, contagious, all the night spitting op blood—yas, deliriums, too, yells like crazy, duh disturbance is something terrific— I wish you would come out here quick and remove him from here. —We pay taxes! [*He hangs up.*]

CHUCK: Mr. Gwendlebaum —!

GWENDLEBAUM: Horry op, git finished yer sveeping. —Duh beds is upstairs to make yet! Leo, you keep sharp account, I'm off to duh Fourteen Street! Windy? Outside is cold, huh? Vere iss my gluffs! Ach, here— Vell keep bizzy [*He crosses out in a great flurry.*]

[*Pete, Rocky and Texas come downstairs.*]

TEXAS: How yuh, Chuck? Merry Xmas! Happy New Year! Powder River! —One mile wide an' six inches deep! [*To Leo:*] Whatcha got here Mr. Collegiate? Aw, yuh college paper —Editor, Leo Gwendlebaum, Jr.! What's this mean? [*He reads*] 'Fascism an' the R.O.T.C.' — Jesus, buddy, are you taken' cracks at the govuhment?

LEO: I'm taking cracks at the compulsory militarization of the American college youth.

TEXAS: Yeah? That's Grand Larceny, boy! How 'bout a checker game, Chuck?

CHUCK: You bet—soon's I git the dorm red up a little.

TEXAS: That's a date, sugah. [*He straddles the bench and twangs his guitar.*] —Say, Chuck, by the way—I got a question to ask you as representin' the management a this here deluxe establishment—

CHUCK: Yeah? What's that?

TEXAS [*grins and scratches*]: Is this here a flophouse or a flea-circus?

[*Everyone laughs. Pete has been scribbling on the wall with a piece of chalk—a cryptic inscription which says for the general enlightenment — "FOO IS FOO."*]

ROCKY: What is Foo?

PETE: What is says here. Foo is foo.

ROCKY: —Yeh, but what *is* Foo, huh?

PETE: Just what it says it is, Foo is Foo, that's what it is, it's just foo! C'mon lunk head—clear your pipes, we're gonna go Chrismuss caroling.

TEXAS [*singing*]:   Me mother is dead and in heaven
                   Me father is gone down below
                   Me sister is gone to join Mo-thurr!
                   An' where I'll go nobody knows! [*Yodels.*]

[*Glory enters, grins, and covers her ears.*]

LEO: I thought Papa told you to stay home?

GLORY: Aw, I finished my washin'. You go on, run along, I got nothing else to do now. —What's these things here? Some more a that Bolshevistic stuff you been writing?

LEO: Let go of that paper!

GLORY: No, I won't—I'm gonna show it to Papa! You'll get kicked out of college if you keep on writing this stuff!

LEO [*wrestling with her*]: Let go of that paper, God damn you!

GLORY: Stop! You're hurting! —Awright! Take it! —But when you get thrown outa school for bein' a Red agitator, you know how Papa's gonna feel about it!

LEO: I know how Papa's gonna feel about it—if I express a few honest opinions! [*He marches out with the bundle under his arm.*]

GLORY [*looking after him proudly*]: Leo's an awful smart kid. Didja see that? His name in print right there at the top a the paper,

Leo Gwendlebaum, Jr., Editor in Chief a the College Clarion!—
[*To a transient shuffling out:*] Hey, you, you owe for three nights.

[*Terry comes quietly down in an overcoat.*]

TRANSIENT: I'm clear on the books.

GLORY: No, you ain't. You owe me for three nights here.

TERRY: That's right buddy. Your bill is forty five cents.

TRANSIENT: Who told you to sound off?

[*Terry steps behind counter and nonchalantly places his revolver on the top of it.*]

TERRY: Me, I don't need to be told nothing.

TRANSIENT [*feebly*]: What the hell is this? A stickup?

[*Terry spins the revolver on the counter.*]

TRANSIENT: All I got's two bits.

[*Terry steps up and frisks the transient. He turns his pockets inside out without finding anything—then suddenly he jerks off the transient's shoe and spills a bunch of coins on the floor.*]

JABE [*coming downstairs*]: By God you hit the jackpot that time!

TERRY [*picking up some coins and flipping them on the counter*]: Now get out quick an' stay out!

[*The transient, grumbling, picks up the rest of the money and shuffles out the door.*]

JABE: You done that like a professional, fellow.

TEXAS: I'll say yuh did.

TERRY: Yeah? Where's the closest hock shop?

TEXAS: Two blocks west on Market. What've you got to hock?

TERRY: Overcoat.

TEXAS: One you got on? That's a nice coat. You oughta get five or six dollars on that.

[*Terry glances at Glory who has watched him with interest during this.*]

TERRY: It cost me sixty.

TEXAS: Whew!

TERRY: Think they'll be open on Christmas?

TEXAS: Sure.

JABE: Them kikes woulden close for the day a Judgment. [*He laughs shrilly.*]

[*Terry goes out.*]

JABE [*shrewdly*]: I didn't know Gwendlebaum kept a gun in the drawer.

GLORY: Sure he does. Why not?

JABE: How did that fellow know it was there?

GLORY: Maybe I told him it was. Anything else you're feeling curious about?

JABE: Me? Naw, I'm not curious about a goddam thing, sister. I'm too sleepy—that lunger kept me awake all night wit' his coughin' an' groanin'—must be gittin ready to cash in his checks. —I told Gwendlebaum to git him outa this place if he wanted to keep my trade.

[*O'Connor, a Federal Agent, enters. He flips a key ring.*]

JABE [*suddenly alert*]: Hello, Mr. O'Connor.

[*Glory goes into the office.*]

O'CONNOR [*to Texas*]: Would you mind getting me a glass a water?

[*Texas looks at him oddly a moment; then goes slowly to a cooler in the back corner of the room.*]

O'CONNOR [*quickly to Jabe*]: Some bum told me a young fellow flashed a gun in here just now.

JABE: That's right.

O'CONNOR: Find out who he is. It might be worth something.

JABE: Sure, Mr. O'Connor.

[*O'Connor goes out.*]

TEXAS [*returning with a paper cup*]: I thought he wanted some water.

JABE: Better drink it yuhself.

TEXAS: Aw, I see. You wouldn't be skunkin' on nobody, would you?

JABE: I never skunk on nobody.

TEXAS: Is that why the coppers love you so much?

JABE: Uh-huh. [*He rises sullenly and goes out.*]

[*Texas strikes a blue chord on his guitar. Olsen comes slowly downstairs.*]

TEXAS: Mawnin', Ole.

[*Olsen looks at him, sits down dully.*]

TEXAS: Hear your partner was took bad sick las' night.

OLSEN: Carl had a bad bleedin' spell. Gwendlebaum's gone an' called up the city hospital. —Carl won't like that.

TEXAS: Naw. He's scared a the hospital, ain't he?

OLSEN: Scared to death. White-coated devils, he calls 'em—he says them amachur sawbones, he calls 'em, feed guys like him to the lab'atory rats!

TEXAS: I heard him talkin' that stuff las' night.

OLSEN: This town's a jinx. I don't like this town. Look out there, that dirty ole muck, that slimy creepin' ole fog all a time—gits down under yer skin, makes yuh sick— He was headed for New Awleens. We woulda made it excep' this cold spell run us in here.

[*Carl appears on the stairs, like a ghost, staggering down, coughing.*]

OLSEN [*springing up*]: Carl!

TEXAS: Carl, boy, what you doin' outa that bed? [*He rises also.*]

CARL [*hoarsely, dragging himself along*]: Don' you all try an' stop me—this town's no good. I'm gittin' outa this town! I'm goin' down the' freight-yards an' catch me a ride outa here!

TEXAS: Naw, you're too sick, old boy, you can't go ridin' the blinds in this kinda weathuh!

OLSEN [*frantically*]: Look here, Carl—

CARL [*yelling*]: Get outa my way, you Swede! —I'd a helluva lot rather die in a ditch wit' buzzards to peck out my eyes than have my bones gnawed by a flock a them stinkin' white rats yer fixin' t' feed me to!

[*An ambulance siren is heard.*]

CARL [*terrified*]: What's that?! [*He retreats a few steps.*]

OLSEN: Now, Carl—

TEXAS: Take it easy there, boy!

CARL [*wildly*]: I know, I know! It's them! You've called 'em! They're comin' to get me! —Yuh double-crossed me, God damn yuh, Swede, yuh lyin', yuh double-crossed me, yuh called 'em, they're comin' t' git me! [*He cringes in terror as the ambulance siren wails louder.*]

[*Glory comes in from office, Gwendlebaum from outside.*]

GLORY: Nobody's gonna hurtcha. They're gonna take care of you, Mister. You'll be in a nice clean bed and won't have to pay for it!

CARL: I'll be in rats' bellies, that's where! [*He screams and darts toward the door—Olsen grabs him, they struggle.*] God damn you, Olsen, you dirty liar, yuh double-crosser! Leggo of me, lemme go now, yuh bastard!

[*Interns enter.*]

OLSEN: Treat him easy, boys, will yuh? He's awful sick, sick in here [*tapping his chest*] an' his head ain't just right from the fever. He'll come around, though, just treat him real easy an' he'll come around okay.

CARL [*collapsing with terror*]: You Girl! [*To Glory:*] Fo' God's sake don' let 'em git me, don' let 'em git me! Please fo' the sake a Jesus! I don't want to die!

INTERN: Steady!

SECOND: All right, fellow, let's go!

[*Carl screams and is borne out struggling.*]

OLSEN: You'll be all right, Carl. You'll be okay in a week— We'll be goin' South befo' long—spend the winter in Florida, Carl!

CARL [*as the door closes*]: God damn you, I'll git you fo' this, if I have to come back out of hell! Damn you, Swede— [*His sobbing and cursing fades out as the door closes.*]

[*Pause—a shocked silence. Olsen drops slowly onto the bench—he looks dazed.*]

GWENDLEBAUM: Vell, dot's how it goes. Here today and tomorrow not here no more. —My head goes in circles. I got so much things to be done! —Vere iss my gluffs? Oh, Gott, I'm losing my gloves! [*He slaps his coat pocket.*] No, here dey are here! At Fourteen Street, broken windows! No I got to get a repairs to fix up—is Leo gone yet?

GLORY: Yes, Papa.

GWENDLEBAUM: I'm going myself again. Vindows git broken, Bush-leaguers, hospitals—goodbye!

OLSEN [*hoarsely*]: You don't think it's true about that?

TEXAS: About what?

OLSEN: Them rats he's scared of.

TEXAS: Naw! —When guys kick off they always git screwy idears.

OLSEN: You think he's—done for?

[*Texas is silent: he rolls a cigarette and offers it to Olsen.*]

OLSEN: Naw, no thanks. [*He rises slowly.*] I'm goin' upstairs.

GLORY: Go up and get some more sleep, Mr. Olsen. There's no extra charge.

[*Olsen climbs slowly out of sight.*]

CHUCK [*brushing past Olsen on stairs*]: Anything more I got to do Glory?

GLORY: No, nothing right now.

CHUCK: That's good. How about that checker game, Texas?

TEXAS: Sure thing. [*He lights the cigarette.*] Get us some music, Glory.

[*Glory switches on the radio. A church choir is heard singing "Carol, Brothers, Carol!"*]

TEXAS [*with sudden violence*]: SHUT IT OFF! [*Pause, he sinks slowly down on bench as Glory switches the radio off.*]

CHUCK [*matter-of-factly*]: Your move, Texas.

[*Texas stares at the board for a moment; then with a single violent motion, he kicks the board off the bench, scattering the checkers, and swerves about, facing the audience, and flings his head down in his hands.*]


CURTAIN

## "YOU OUGHT TO WEAR BRIGHT COLORS"

*It is the evening of December 28. Lounging about the lobby are Texas, Jabe, Pete and Rocky. Pete is scribbling on the wall with his piece of chalk—"Foo Plus Foo is Foo."*

ROCKY: Now I know what 'foo' is.

PETE: What is it?

ROCKY: It's nothin'.

PETE: What makes yuh think it's nothin'?

ROCKY: Cause nothin' is the only thing that would be the same thing when you added the same things to it. That's plain arithmetic.

PETE: What do you know about arithmetic?

ROCKY: I took it when I went to school once.

PETE: Foo is foo, that's what it is, it's just foo. —Lookit what's standin' outside!

*[Bertha has appeared at the window, looking inside speculatively. She is a frowzy blond prostitute about thirty-five.]*

JABE *[sauntering over to the door]*: It's that ole snowbird* again. *[He opens the door.]* Hello, Bertha.

BERTHA *[entering]*: How yuh, Skunk. I smelt somethin' rotten around here a minute ago but I thought maybe it was just the

---

* Snowbird— A user of cocaine.

wind from over the packin' house. [*She winks at Texas.*] I didn't know Jabe was in town.

JABE [*visibly stung*]: Still crackin' wise, huh?

BERTHA: You know it! [*Approaching Texas.*] Who's the big boy?

TEXAS: Howdy, Ma'am.

JABE: Gwendlebaum don't allow no hustling in here.

BERTHA [*with shrill laughter*]: Hustling? Where does he pick up them funny words! —I don't know what I'd refer to you as, Jabe Stallcup, but you certainly ain't what we know as a gentleman down our way.

JABE: Pretty high tonight, ain't you?

BERTHA: Sure, toots. I'm floating around Pike's Peak. What's it to you?

JABE: I thought you took the cure.

BERTHA: They had me strapped in bed seven weeks las' summer in the psychopathic ward—if you call that a cure! Where's that little fellow works here?

JABE: Chuck? He's sweepin' upstairs. —Where do you get your stuff from, Bertha?

BERTHA: Oh, sure, you'd like to know so you could spill it to the Government, wouldn't you, sweetheart?

[*Chuck comes downstairs.*]

BERTHA: Well, hello, Stranger!

CHUCK: Hi, Bertha, how's tricks?

BERTHA: So-so. Where you been keepin' yourself?

CHUCK: Right here on the job.

BERTHA: Why don'tcha drop in ever?

CHUCK: Well, I—

BERTHA: I know, you're broke, aintcha?

CHUCK: I been hopin' we'd have a good snow this week so's I could pick up a little money out West End with my shovel.

[*Pete and Rocky laugh.*]

JABE: Bertha's got plenty of snow up at her place, buddy.

BERTHA: How do you know? I never let you in. [*To Texas:*] I sure do like guitar music.

JABE: There's your opportunity, Texas.

BERTHA: Texas? Oh, you're from the South. Me, too, I'm from Memphis.

JABE: I bet the Memphis Chamber of Commerce would pay you fifty bucks for ev'ry time yo forgot to mention that fact.

BERTHA: That's what you think. How about it, Texas?

TEXAS: Sorry lady, no sale tonight. [*He strikes a blues chord on the guitar.*]

BERTHA: Broke?

TEXAS: Uh-huh.

BERTHA: That's a good-lookin' tie pin you got on. [*She fingers his horseshoe pin.*]

TEXAS: I keep that for good luck.

BERTHA: Well, I hope it brings you plenty, sweet boy. [*To Pete and Rocky:*] How 'bout you freshwaters?

PETE [*grinning at Rocky*]: Huh?

ROCKY: Uh-huh!

JABE: I'd have to need a woman a hell of a lot worse'n I do now before I'd go sleighridin'* with her.

BERTHA [*furiously*]: Say, you!

JABE: Huh?

BERTHA: I may be old and I may be cheap—Yes, and I may be jazzed all to hell an' gone in a blizzard of snow! —But I'll be damned if I'd ever squawk to coppers!

JABE: Git out.

BERTHA: Don't you worry, I'm gittin'.

PETE: Let's go, Rocky.

BERTHA: See you when it snows, Chuck. Toodle-oo!

---

* Sleighridin'— A cocaine party, possibly with sexual overtones.

[*She goes out with the two boys.*]

TEXAS [*grinning*]: She had you told!

[*O'Connor, the Federal Agent, enters.*]

JABE: Hello, Mr. O'Connor.

TEXAS: How 'bout some water, Mr. O'Connor?

O'CONNOR: No, thanks.

[*Texas goes out strumming.*]

O'CONNOR: What do you know?

JABE: Nothing much.

O'CONNOR: I mean about the guy I mentioned the other day.

JABE: I know. But I can't get nothing out of him. All he does is sit in a corner with a newspaper up in front of his puss.

O'CONNOR: Don't talk to nobody?

JABE: Nobody but Gwendlebaum's girl.

O'CONNOR: One that works here?

JABE: Yeah. There's somethin' between 'em. She's always been cagey's a rabbit but with him she's—

O'CONNOR: Sweet on him?

JABE: You oughta see how they look at each other!

O'CONNOR: That's an angle for you to work on.

JABE: That's what I thought.

O'CONNOR: Even the best of 'em slip on a skirt sometimes. What name does he give?

JABE: None that I know of.

O'CONNOR: Find out from the girl. We're lookin' for a boy named Meighan.

JABE [*impressed*]: Terry Meighan? Why didn't you say so before!

O'CONNOR: We haven't got much to go on. Not even a picture. All we got is a general description.

JABE: Does it fit this guy?

O'CONNOR: Not exactly. Terry's known for being a gent. Dresses fancy an' stops at first-class hotels.

JABE: This guy's broke. Pawned his overcoat Xmas mornin' when you seen him go out.

O'CONNOR: What shop?

JABE: Goldman's at Fourteenth and Market.

O'CONNOR: What name did he sign on the slip?

JABE: I couldn't get nothing out of Goldman.

O'CONNOR: I'll check that myself. You work on the girl, that's your angle.

[*Gwendlebaum enters.*]

JABE: You leave it to me, Mr. O'Connor.

[*O'Connor goes out.*]

GWENDLEBAUM [*agitated*]: Glory! Hey, Glory! Vere's da girl?

CHUCK [*coming downstairs.*]: She ain't here, Mr. Gwendlebaum. She went round the corner to git a haircut at the beauty shop at the Ritz Hotel.

GWENDLEBAUM: Haircut, Beauty shop, Ritz! Neffer heard soch a ting! Didn't I leaf her in charge?

CHUCK: She said for me to take care of the desk while she's gone.

GWENDLEBAUM: You! —Vell, neffer mind. I go fetch her back here myself—beauty shop, haircut, Ritz!

[*He exits hastily. After a few moments Terry enters, seats himself with newspaper. Jabe watches him a while and then approaches him.*]

JABE [*offering tobacco pouch*]: Have some makin's?

TERRY: No, thanks.

JABE: I guess you're used to tailor mades.

[*Terry turns page without comment.*]

JABE: You know, I'm tryin' to place you ever since I first seen you here. I met you somewheres before. Oh, now I know! You been in Detroit, ain't you?

TERRY: No.

JABE: No? That's sure funny. I coulda sworn I'd seen you in Detroit not long ago.

TERRY: Well, it's a good thing you didn't perjure yourself. I never been east of the river.

JABE: That's funny all right. I coulda sworn—

[*Glory enters.*]

JABE: Hello, Glory.

GLORY [*shortly*]: Hello.

JABE: You look mighty sweet tonight.

GLORY: Thanks.

JABE: Your old man was just looking for you.

GLORY: I just saw him.

JABE: Must think you got nothing to do with yourself but hang around here. Girl your age, your looks, should be stepping out places or working some place decent.

[*Glory steps into the office and removes her hat before the mirror.*]

JABE: Wouldn't be having a date tonight?

GLORY: No.

JABE: Just giving the customers a break! [*He laughs and goes upstairs.*]

[*Glory comes out of the office and goes to the counter.*]

TERRY: Who is that rat?

GLORY: They call him Jabe, I think.

TERRY: I don't like his looks.

GLORY: I don't think it's his looks that he's been getting by on.

TERRY: I don't either. [*He rises and stirs restlessly about the room.*] I guess I oughta start moving. This is the longest I stayed in one place for some time.

GLORY: What's holding you then?

TERRY: Right now I got no place to go. Waiting to get word from somebody. A friend of mine with connections.

GLORY: You could find a better place to wait.

TERRY: How do you mean?

GLORY: Oh, nothing. [*She walks slowly over to the bench and picks up a magazine. She seats herself.*]

TERRY [*watching her avidly*]: This place has got at least one big attraction.

GLORY: Has it? [*She self-consciously arranges her skirt.*] I guess I oughta pretend like I was real modest and not get the point.

TERRY: You know what I mean all right. [*His intent stare makes her uncomfortable.*]

GLORY: What's wrong?

TERRY: Huh?

GLORY: Have I got a run in my stocking or something?

TERRY: Oh. [*He laughs.*] Your stocking's all right, but I don't like your dress.

GLORY: Oh, you're criticizing my clothes, are you, mister!

TERRY: You oughta wear bright colors.

GLORY: Think so?

TERRY: Red's my favorite color.

[*He leans back with narrowed eyes. Glory stiffens and looks away.*]

TERRY: I like to see girls dressed in red.

GLORY: Red's loud.

TERRY: That's what I like about red. [*He rises and moves toward her.*] Builds a girl up. Sort of—emphasizes all her good points.

GLORY [*uncertainly*]: Brown's more—practical—for business.

TERRY: You ain't the practical type.

GLORY: You've got my type and everything have you?

TERRY: No, not everything yet.

GLORY: Considering the length of our acquaintance it seems to me that you take a lot for granted!

TERRY: I'm not taking nothing for granted. Some girls need to hide themselves behind colors like you got on so they won't be noticed but what you need's publicity! What do you wrap yourself up in that gunny sack for?

GLORY [*furiously*]: What?

TERRY: That thing you got on! I should think you'd rather go naked!

[*They stand facing each other, trembling, as though engaged in a violent quarrel. Suddenly they both realize the incongruity of it and retreat a few steps.*]

GLORY: What do you—what do you mean by that?

TERRY: Sorry, I—I don't know what I got all steamed up about!

GLORY [*avoiding his eyes*]: I'm sure I don't either.

TERRY [*sinking dejectedly on bench*]: I guess it's just that I—

GLORY: Had any supper?

TERRY: Yes.

GLORY: What are you bothered about?

TERRY: That guy Jabe—

GLORY: Oh. Him.

TERRY: He asks too many questions—I got a notion he's good at answering, too.

GLORY: He wanted to know what your name was last night.

TERRY: Tell him?

GLORY: How could I tell him? I didn't know.

TERRY: I've kinda got outa the habit of introducin' myself.

GLORY: No reason for it in here.

TERRY: I guess it's hard to even remember their faces with so many going and coming.

GLORY: Some faces it's hard to remember and some it ain't.

TERRY [*looking up with a slight smile*]: How about mine?

GLORY [*looking away*]: Oh, I don't know. —Maybe I've seen a few that—that I could forget about quicker.

TERRY [*pause*]: I won't forget yours.

GLORY [*with abrupt movement*]: That's nice.

TERRY: What else did Jabe want to know?

GLORY: Just your name.

TERRY: Didn't you mention the piece of hardware we stashed in the drawer?

GLORY: No. But he was suspicious about it when you took it out to frisk that bum Xmas morning.

TERRY: I know. That was a fool thing to do—Anderson's my name if anyone asks. What's yours?

GLORY: I don't know. Papa Gwendlebaum used to know, but he couldn't pronounce it so it just slipped his mind.

TERRY: Huh?

GLORY: My folks was Armenians.

TERRY: What become of 'em?

GLORY: Mother died over there. My father he jumped off the boat coming over.

TERRY: How did you get mixed up with the Gwendlebaums?

GLORY: They was on the same boat. Me an' Leo played together a lot so—

TERRY: Gwendlebaum adopted you?

GLORY: Yes. He called me Glory for the American flag.

TERRY [*smiling*]: Glory for the American flag! —So Leo ain't your real brother, huh? —You ain't stuck on him, are you?

GLORY: No. What makes you ask?

TERRY: Curiosity.

GLORY: That's what killed the cat.

TERRY: It won't kill me. [*He glances at the paper.*] Garbo's at the Palace tomorrow. You wanta go?

GLORY: I don't go running around to picture shows with whoever asks me.

TERRY: Don't you go out on dates?

GLORY: I don't see that's your concern.

TERRY: Excuse me. Maybe you'd rather I kept my mouth shut. Want me to go up to bed?

GLORY: Customers are allowed to stay in the lobby till twelve.

TERRY: Thanks.

GLORY: For what?

TERRY: It's lonesome up there.

GLORY: We got sixteen beds taken up.

TERRY: I still say it's lonesome.

[*Enter Texas, Pete and Rocky, hurriedly, stamping cold feet. Rocky straggles behind in his usual slow-witted fashion. Texas is in the middle of a tirade against a mechanistic world.*]

TEXAS: Radios an' electric-victrolas, machine-music, that's all they want, these lousy clip-joints around here! What chance does a flesh'n blood artist got against them? That place over there on Sixteenth, for instance, the one where the—

PETE [*approaching stove.*]: Christ, how I could honey up to this baby if it was only a blond!

TEXAS: Come on! [*He winks at Glory.*] It looks like we're making a crowd! [*He and Pete go upstairs.*]

ROCKY [*pulling bundled paper from inside coat.*]: Cold outside!

GLORY: Yes.

ROCKY: It sure is cold. [*He clumps slowly upstairs.*]

TERRY [*when they have gone*]: Window's all frosted over. Can't hardly see through it. —Don't you ever get nervous in here at night?

GLORY: No.

TERRY: Not even hearin' them talk about women like that?

GLORY: Oh, that's only just kid stuff.

TERRY [*smiling*]: I'm not exactly a kid. We're in here alone.

GLORY [*sharply*]: Listen! I'm getting tired of you making those kind of remarks!

[*She goes to the counter. He steps behind her and clasps her shoulders tightly.*]

GLORY: What's that for?

TERRY: For you to know me a little better, that's all. Sometimes people need to stand close together like this so as to feel the truth in each other.

[*Glory's face is to the audience, averted from Terry. An inner struggle is apparent.*]

GLORY: Let go of me, please.

TERRY [*sensing her divided emotion*]: You don't want me to!

GLORY: I want you to let me go!

TERRY: No, you don't. [*He smiles.*] You can't lie to a man when he's got his hands on your body. He can feel the truth inside you. It runs through his fingers.

GLORY: It you don't let me go I'll—

[*Chuck enters. Glory and Terry break quickly apart. Terry whistles and looks out the window, his hands in his pockets.*]

CHUCK: Turnin' colder tonight.

GLORY [*confused*]: Yes.

CHUCK: You think there's a chance it might snow?

[*Terry laughs with abrupt violence, relieving his pent-up emotion. Glory, in spite of herself, laughs also.*]

CHUCK: What's funny?

GLORY: Nothing. I was thinking about something else. [*She looks sharply at Terry.*]

CHUCK [*opening the door to appraise the weather*]: If I had six bits I'd git my shovel out of hock. [*He goes back upstairs.*]

TERRY [*earnestly*]: You think there's a chance it might snow?

GLORY: Smart! [*Pause.*]

TERRY: I wish it would snow myself.

GLORY: Why? Would you get your shovel out of hock, too?

TERRY: No, I'd just lay in bed an' listen to it.

GLORY: Listen to it? You can't hear snow.

TERRY: Sure you can, if you listen. It makes a good sound—I like snow.

GLORY: Do you?

TERRY: It does big things for a neighborhood like this.

GLORY: How's that?

TERRY: Covers things up! Makes everything look clean an' decent an' — stuff like that!

GLORY: Gosh. Fellows like you don't often make such poetic remarks about snow! Sounds more like Leo—he says things like that.

TERRY [*resentfully*]: Going to college gives you more right to say what you please?

GLORY: No, it gives you less right. Leo gets in trouble at college for saying too much what he pleases. The Dean asked him, Leo, what do you want to do, reform the world or get a degree from this University?

TERRY: What did Leo say?

GLORY: He said he thought reforming the world was a more important piece of business.

TERRY: That's bad. You tell your kid brother for me that the world's a hopeless case. It's like galloping consumption—the only cure is the axe!

[*A police siren is heard outside. Terry rises quickly and crosses to the stairs, his hands moving mechanically to his inside pocket.*]

GLORY: What's the matter?

[*The siren fades.*]

TERRY: Nothing. [*He grins with relief.*] Loud noise makes me nervous sometimes. [*He rubs clear a small space on the frosted window.*] I like these windows of yours when they're frosted this way—you can rub off just enough to see out without being seen.

GLORY: Is that an advantage?

TERRY: From my point of view. Makes it more intimate-like.

[*A transient passes through.*]

TRANSIENT: Cold night out.

TERRY: It's clear.

[*The transient goes upstairs.*]

TERRY: I can see the clock on the Grand Terminal Tower. I can even tell the time—it's eleven-thirty. —There's a bunch of stars right over the tower. One of them big constellations. I'd like to know more about them kind of things. D'you know— [*He laughs.*] —I never found out till just a couple of years ago that they don't have five points on 'em. I always thought they was like them silver things that sissies at St. Anne's Parish used to cut out an' stick on Xmas trees. I never had time to find out about things like that, when I was a kid. I was too busy swiping from vegetable carts or dodging the tough boys in the neighborhood gang. Grab an' run, that was me, all the time. Just think what a lot of things a guy could find out if he just had the time an' the money!

GLORY: Well, you've got plenty of time.

TERRY: Maybe I have.

GLORY: Why shouldn't you have? You're young and you look pretty healthy to me.

TERRY: I might catch a disease or something.

GLORY: A disease?

TERRY: You never can tell. There's lots of germs floating around that I ain't been vaccinated against.

GLORY: If you was smart you'd stay out of their way.

TERRY: Staying out of their way's my profession, lady.

[*More transients enter, their coats padded with newspapers for warmth. They scatter papers about the floor and pay for beds.*]

TERRY: Good business tonight.

GLORY: When it drops below thirty business always picks up. Those fellows live in boxes along the river. [*She stoops to pick up the papers.*]

TERRY: Here—let me do that.

[*Their shoulders touch—involuntarily they rise and face each other.*]

TERRY [*hoarsely after a pause.*]: What is it between you and me?

GLORY [*defensively*]: Nothing that I know of.

TERRY: I seen it a while ago when you was looking at me.

GLORY: You mean when you spouted that screwy stuff about snow? Sure. I thought how funny you were!

TERRY: It wasn't just then. It was now when I touched your hand, and it was a while ago when I had my hands on your shoulders.

GLORY: Some people's nerve is surprising!

TERRY: I felt it before then, too. I felt it the first night I come in here when you give me that four bits and I let you keep my rod. You could have turned me over to cops that night. It might have been worth your while. But you didn't!

GLORY: No, I didn't. Maybe that was my mistake!

TERRY: You know it wasn't. It was because—

GLORY: Because what?

TERRY: You felt something between me and you the same as I felt.

GLORY: You ain't half conceited, are you?

TERRY: That ain't conceit. I don't flatter myself that I'm a knockout with all the dames.

GLORY: I must say that's modest of you.

TERRY: Why don't you lay off the hard talk? You ain't like that underneath. You're quiet underneath.

GLORY: Quiet!?

TERRY [*his voice trembling slightly*]: Yes, you're quiet underneath. You're quiet. I need that. I've never been quiet inside. I've been crazy, wild. I've done things without stopping to think, like I was driven by something, everything splitting and crashing around me like trees in a storm. I'll tell you the truth. I was scared. That's why I ducked for the stairs just now when that wagon went by. I was scared—

GLORY: You think you're telling me something?

TERRY: No. You already knew it.

GLORY: From the minute you showed me that yellow-back bill.

TERRY: But that didn't make no difference.

GLORY: What?

TERRY: You wanted me just the same.

GLORY: Wanted you!?

TERRY: You did. You're lonesome like me.

GLORY: Lonesome? I get around all right!

TERRY: That don't keep you from being lonesome. You ain't met the guy you could care for. Not till—

GLORY: Haven't I? That's all you know. I happen to be going steady right now.

TERRY: Steady?

GLORY: Yes—steady!

TERRY [*after pause*]: I'd like to meet him.

GLORY: He calls for me every night at a quarter of twelve—right here.

TERRY: Good—I'll take a look at him.

GLORY [*sarcastically*]: To see if you approve?

TERRY: Yes.

GLORY: Maybe he wouldn't approve of you.

TERRY: I'm damned sure of that.

GLORY [*with a flare of anger*]: You should be. If he known that I was associating with—

TERRY: The criminal class?

GLORY: I want you to get this straight. There's nothing personal between you and me. There ain't gonna be. And the sooner you get out of here the better I'll like it. Yes, I've got your number. You're a crook. I oughta turn you over to the police, and why I don't, I don't know! But it ain't because I'm stuck on you. I want you to understand that.

[*A pause, they face each other, shaking.*]

TERRY [*slowly*]: I guess you said enough.

[*He pulls on his hat and turns up his coat collar. He goes slowly outside. Glory watches him go. Then she turns out one of the lights and goes slowly behind the counter and starts to put on her hat. Then, with a choked sob, she suddenly flings her hands over her face. Herman appears dimly through the frosted window: raps with coin on the pane. Glory quickly straightens herself. Herman raps again impatiently and flattens his nose against window, peering in.*]

GLORY: Coming, Herman! Coming!

[*Dabbing her face with powder, she rushes out to join him. We hear a truck rumbling down the street or a clanging streetcar—*]

CURTAIN

## "BEANSTALK COUNTRY"

*It is the next evening, December 29, about eleven-thirty. Chuck passes through lobby. He pauses at the office door.*

CHUCK: Glory?

GLORY [*inside*]: Yes?

CHUCK [*blowing his nose*]: I'm gonna turn in.

GLORY: All right. I'll wait for Papa.

[*Chuck goes upstairs. Terry enters from outside and begins to read the newspaper in his customary corner. Glory comes out of the office. She is wearing a red dress and appears nervous. Terry ignores her.*]

GLORY: Hello. [*Pause.*] I said, "Hello."

TERRY: Uh-huh. I heard you.

GLORY: Mad about last night?

TERRY: No. Forget it. —How long till you close up?

GLORY: About half'n hour. —Why?

TERRY: I'm expecting somebody. A weasel-face guy with a little mustache. Anybody like that been in here?

GLORY: Not anybody by that description. [*She tears a page off the wall calendar.*] It's almost the end of the year. —I'm sorry about last night. Maybe I was a little too—

TERRY: Why worry about it?

[*Drake enters. Glory goes back into the office.*]

TERRY: Sit down.

DRAKE [*seating himself beside Terry*]: This is the last place I'd expect to find *you*.

TERRY: That's why I'm here.

DRAKE: Not much privacy about it.

TERRY: I'm not looking for privacy. In a crowd one guy more or less ain't so conspicuous.

DRAKE: Depends on the guy.

TERRY: You mean I'm a stand-out?

DRAKE: You can't make a sow's ear out of a silk purse, Terry.

TERRY: Thanks. I want to get out of this joint. That's why I called you up. Joe Spitalni said I should call you if I needed anything here.

DRAKE: That was nice of Joe, but—

TERRY: I'm not asking for a handout. I don't expect nothing for nothing from nobody!

DRAKE: That's sensible of you, Meighan.

TERRY: I'm not using that name. Call me Anderson.

DRAKE: What's the proposition, Anderson?

TERRY: You know what I've got.

DRAKE: Not exactly. Bank notes or bonds?

TERRY: Both.

DRAKE: Tch-tch. That heist you pulled in Detroit?

TERRY: Sure.

DRAKE: That was a bad job, Terry. A smart operator don't have to use irons.

TERRY: I didn't even carry one on that job. I was just a sort of technical advisor.

DRAKE: You were *particeps criminis.**

TERRY: Whatever that means.

DRAKE: It means they could jerk you to Jesus for that or any one a them jobs you pulled out East. —I guess the Syndicate turned you down cold this time.

TERRY: They offered us forty per cent.

DRAKE: Think I'm a two-year-old?

TERRY: What do you mean?

DRAKE: I mean the Syndicate didn't offer you any forty per cent

---

* *Particeps criminis*—An accomplice in crime.

on that paper. I was with the Syndicate before you graduated from reform school.

TERRY: Never went to reform school. What's your offer?

DRAKE: Ten per cent.

TERRY: Now it's my turn to laugh!

DRAKE: Ten per cent.

TERRY: Ten cents on the dollar! You think that— !

DRAKE: Ten per cent! [*He starts to rise.*]

TERRY: Sit down—ten per cent! That would give Joe Spitalni a laugh. Look at this.

DRAKE: Look at what?

TERRY: Personal Column. [*He points.*] That's from Joe. "Can put up a fence for thirty." You've got to beat that, Drake.

DRAKE [*shrugging*]: Oh, you want to go back East, do you?

TERRY: No, I don't wanta go back East. That's why I called you.

DRAKE: You wouldn't go back!

TERRY: I'm good at taking chances!

DRAKE: Who is this changer of Joe's?

TERRY: He's all right or Joe wouldn't be dealing with him.

DRAKE: It don't change my offer. You don't know how hot you are, Meighan.

TERRY: Anderson, I toleja.

DRAKE: Everything you touch is hot, so hot that it sizzles. Can't you see that newspaper turning brown around the edges?

TERRY: Shut up, God damn you! [*He throws the paper aside.*]

DRAKE: I don't blame you for being nervous.

TERRY [*shoving him*]: Go on, weasel—crawl back into your hole! I don't wanta do business with you anyhow.

GLORY [*entering from the office*]: Closing up in a minute.

DRAKE: All right. I was just leaving. —Mr. Anderson, you know my number.

TERRY: Yes, I got your number!

DRAKE: Good night. [*He bows suavely and leaves. Terry rises slowly and goes to the counter.*]

GLORY: Anything the matter?

TERRY: No, nothing's the matter. [*He pauses on the stairs.*] What difference would it make to you anyhow?

GLORY: None that I know of.

TERRY: I notice you got on a red dress tonight.

GLORY: I got it for Christmas. No reason why I shouldn't wear it.

TERRY: It looks good on you.

GLORY: I suppose you think I'm wearin' it for your benefit.

TERRY: Oh, no. You told me where I stood last night.

GLORY: I'm glad you remember.

TERRY: Are you? [*He grins*] How much do I owe?

GLORY: Checking out?

TERRY: Tomorrow morning. [*He counts the change from his pocket.*] Five times fifteen—

GLORY: Six bits.

TERRY: I'll trouble you now for the security I give you.

[*Leo enters, disheveled.*]

GLORY [*surprised at his appearance*]: Leo!

TERRY: Wrap it up and I'll call for it in the morning. [*He crosses upstairs.*]

LEO: Yes. I guess I look pretty awful.

GLORY: What's happened?

LEO: This afternoon I got—kicked out of school.

GLORY: Leo! No!

LEO: Yes, that's what happened. [*He touches his forehead which is bruised.*]

GLORY: What's the matter with your face? You're hurt!

LEO [*slowly*]: I must've—knocked up against something.

GLORY: It's bleeding. Leo, did somebody hit you? Who were you fighting with, Leo?

LEO: Fighting? Nobody. I just bumped against something.

GLORY: Where? When did this happen? Leo, tell me!

LEO: I just told you. This afternoon I got kicked out of school.

GLORY: Oh, Leo, I don't mean that. That don't matter so much.

LEO: Don't matter?

GLORY: I mean the cut on your forehead.

LEO: I bumped against a street lamp.

GLORY: Leo!

LEO: I'm so disgusted—such a fool! Why couldn't I keep my mouth shut?

GLORY: That's what Papa and me kept warning you to do— Sit down, Leo. I'll put something on that cut. [*She gets a wet towel and washes his face.*]

LEO: Where's Papa?

GLORY: Fourteenth Street.

LEO: Will he come here?

GLORY: To close up.

LEO: I don't want to see him. —I can't see him, Glory.

GLORY: Don't be a fool. Papa will—he'll understand.

LEO: No, he won't. I'm not anymore his son than you're his daughter.

GLORY: That don't sound nice. Papa's been terribly proud of you—him and me both, we expect you to be a big success.

LEO: A big success! You mean you want me to stick my fist down as deep as I can in the grab bag and pull out all I can get hold of!

GLORY: No, I don't mean that.

LEO: Papa does. That's his idea of a big success.

GLORY: No, Leo, he wants you to be—

LEO: What?

GLORY: Happy.

LEO: How could anybody be happy in a system like this?

GLORY: I wish you'd stop talking like that. That's what's got you in trouble at school.

LEO: I talked too much.

GLORY: I knew you would. [*She presses the cloth to his head.*] Hold still. Let this stay on the swelling a while.

LEO [*closing his eyes*]: You know I've got to get out.

GLORY: Don't be silly.

LEO: I can't stay home like this.

GLORY: You're feverish, ain't you?

LEO: Why don't we go off someplace together.

GLORY: Where?

LEO: Anywhere!

GLORY: Yes, you've got fever.

LEO: I don't know. I feel all confused. Broken up inside.

GLORY [*seeing Gwendlebaum through window*]: Here comes Papa.

LEO: Oh, Lord!

GLORY: Now try and keep hold of yourself. Let me tell him in the morning, Leo—

[*Gwendlebaum enters.*]

GLORY [*with false brightness*]: Hello, Papa.

GWENDLEBAUM [*starting with surprise*]: Vot are you doink here diss time a night?

[*Leo doesn't answer.*]

GWENDLEBAUM: Vot's da matter vit him, is he seek or sometink?

GLORY: Leave him alone a while, Papa. He'll tell you about it later.

LEO [*tensely*]: No, I'll tell you now. I'm not afraid. I've got nothing to be ashamed of—Papa, I've— [*His courage breaks and he averts his face.*] I've been expelled from the university!

GWENDLEBAUM [*in a hushed tone*]: Ek-shpelled! —Glory, vot does he mean?

GLORY: Well, Papa, Leo's been—

LEO: Kicked out! Don't you understand? Kicked out!

GWENDLEBAUM [*agonized*]: But vhy? But vhy? [*Neither speaks.*] Kicked out from collich. No, it ain't possible. [*His voice rises.*] You vouldn't dare to come here and tell me a tink like dot after all dot I've—

GLORY: Papa, now—

GWENDLEBAUM: It's true, den?

GLORY: Yes, it's true, Papa. Leo says—

GWENDLEBAUM: Let him speak for himself. Ain't he man enough even for dot?

GLORY: Now leave him be, Papa. Let him tell you about it later. He's not well, he's got a fever.

GWENDLEBAUM: Oh, Gott! I hope de dead haven't got ears dot your mudder should hear soch a tink! A disgrace like dis. Kicked out. Not graduated, not efen just quit—but kicked out! —How did diss happen? You answer me, by God, or I'll—

GLORY: Papa!

LEO: I'll tell you but you won't understand.

GWENDLEBAUM: It's diss radicalism. Dot's vot it iss. I tought after da Dean gaf you dot varning you promised me you vouldn't stir up no more trouble. But no! Your fadder's vishes are not of any himportance. Vot I done, my sacrifices to make you a place in da vorld vas no goot! You trow dem avay because you can't keep your trap shut about tinks vich are none of your bitzness! —Vhy don't you speak?

GLORY: It's that paper at school that Leo's been writing for, Papa.

GWENDLEBAUM: Oh, der paper. I suppose you said, 'Down vit capitalism!' — 'Hooray for da Revolution!' — or sometink like dot! Don't y'know it's capitalism dot keeps dot university goink? Vy should da Board of Trustees put up vit writinks like dot! —So dey kicked you out of da collich?

LEO: They took away my scholarship.

GWENDLEBAUM [*with desperate gesture*]: Took avay your scholarship! How do you tink you can afford to go on vitout your scholarship?

LEO [*violently*]: I don't want to go on—I'm leaving home!

GWENDLEBAUM: Leaving—?

GLORY: No, Leo, you can't do that. Papa will find some way—

LEO: I won't be a burden on him.

GWENDLEBAUM: He's right about that. I'm all vashed up vit him now. Nahhhh! [*He turns away.*] All I can do is tank Gott his mudder ain't here to vitness diss dradful disgrace!

[*The following speeches continue in staccato mode.*]

LEO: If it's a disgrace to have a social conscience—

GWENDLEBAUM: Social — shot op!

LEO: No, by God, I won't! I've got something inside me—

GWENDLEBAUM: Vords, vords, more vords!

LEO: That won't let me keep my trap shut like smart little Jewish boys should—

GWENDLEBAUM: Vere do you tink you'll get vit dot stoff?

LEO: Oh, I know what side my bread's buttered on. I oughta kow-tow to the reactionaries—

GWENDLEBAUM: Reactions! Yass, yass! Social, capital! Go on vit yer ravink.

LEO: Then they'd renew my scholarship and give me—

GWENDLEBAUM: Your scholarship's gone!

LEO: A nice piece of sheepskin this spring—

GWENDLEBAUM: Nahhhh!

LEO: With my name in beautiful gold-engraved letters—

GWENDLEBAUM: All gone! Trown away like a—

LEO: But I made the mistake of—

GWENDLEBAUM: Shooting your trap off! Shooting your God damn —

LEO: Telling the truth, and so I'm—

GWENDLEBAUM: *Keeked out*! [*Pause.*]

LEO [*turning away*]: Yes that's the story.

[*Both of them are panting.*]

GWENDLEBAUM [*hoarsely*]: Vot *ISS* it you vant? Communism?

LEO: No, I don't want Communism, I want—

GWENDLEBAUM: Vot *iss* it you vant? See!? You don't know!

GLORY: Oh, Papa—

GWENDLEBAUM: You're chust vot dey call a—conscientious obchector! You don't know vot it iss you're obchectink against, you're chust obchectink!

LEO: Stop it!

GLORY: Leave him be, Papa.

LEO: I can't stand anymore of it.

GWENDLEBAUM: Vot do you intend to do vit yourself? Moon around home writink papers?

LEO: No!

GWENDLEBAUM: Den vot?

LEO: I told you I'm leaving—I'll find a place for myself.

GWENDLEBAUM: No vhere! All you vish to do is destroy! Tear down! Dere is no place for you, Leo.

LEO: You think I'm damned? —A radical Jew without money? —Maybe you're right—

GWENDLEBAUM: A radical—yass!

LEO: Yes, all I've got is my indignation. [*He laughs harshly.*] And what does indignation get you? A kick in the face!

GWENDLEBAUM [*shaking his fists with the vehemence of a Hebrew prophet, his face contorted*]: LOCK OPP! [*He slams his fists on his thighs and shakes his head. Then he moves slowly to the office, exhausted.*] —Lock opp . . . . [*He shuts his office door.*]

LEO [*turning to Glory*]: I'm going now, Glory.

GLORY: Leo, don't do anything foolish. You stay down here tonight and in the morning—

LEO: No, I'm going.

GLORY: Where?

LEO [*toward window*]: There's lots of places!

GLORY: But Leo—

LEO: I'm not sorry this happened. [*He continues with feverish excitement.*] I was sick of being shut up in that tight little box of a world!

GLORY: Leo, you wanted to get your degree so's you could—

LEO: I don't want that now. What's a degree but a piece of paper? The world's all cluttered up with pieces of paper already. They don't mean much. I want something that's— [*He concludes his expression with a vague, comprehensive gesture that seems to include the whole universe.*]

GWENDLEBAUM [*emerging grimly from office*]: Glory, ve're locking opp now.

GLORY: Yes.

LEO [*as Gwendlebaum goes upstairs*]: Glory, why don't you come with me? We've always stuck together.

GLORY: I know but—Leo, I couldn't. —Oh, I'm not satisfied neither. I'd like to get out of this box that I'm caught in, too, but— I owe it to Papa, his taking me in and all—

LEO: You've paid him back double, slaving down here in this— Glory—you aren't afraid of it, are you?

GLORY: Afraid of what?

LEO [*going to the window*]: The city out there.

GLORY: No. Why should I be?

LEO: Look at those towers out there! What's bigger—me or them?

GLORY: Leo! What do you mean?

LEO: Remember on the boat coming over how both of us cried when we saw New York from the deck? I caught hold of your hand and wouldn't let go till Papa promised that you would come along with us!

GLORY: Yes, I remember that—I cried because I'd lost—father.

LEO: I cried because I was scared of America. [*He laughs.*] It looked so fantastically—big. Like the country at the top of the beanstalk! I was sure that all of the people in it would be giants and ogres. I guess I'm still slightly scared. But now I'm going to climb up to the top of that beanstalk and show 'em that I'm—a giant-killer!

GLORY [*maternally*]: Leo, you ain't ready for climbing that beanstalk yet.

LEO: If I'm not I'll get smashed trying!

GWENDLEBAUM [*coming back downstairs*]: Leo! —Here iss some money.

LEO: No, I don't want your money!

GWENDLEBAUM: Vot are you goink to do? Be a bum?

LEO [*violently*]: I can take care of myself. —Good-bye. [*He goes quickly out the door.*]

GLORY: Leo! —Papa, don't let him!

GWENDLEBAUM [*after pause*]: Da young—fool! —He can take care of himself.

GLORY [*sobbing*]: You should've stopped him!

GWENDLEBAUM: Don't worry. [*He extinguishes the overhead light.*] He ain't gone for good. [*He awkwardly touches her shoulder.*] You vouldn't belief it to look at me now but ven I vas his ach I vass de vay dot he iss. I tought the whole world vas wrong egcep me und dot I vass right absolutely. I tought it vas up to me to mak de whole vorld offer again— D'you know vot iss wrong vit him, Glory? De boy iss an optimist! Yass, he's a great optimist! He tinks it iss possible for men nod too fight vit each udder!— [*He wraps himself in a woolen reefer and turns out the back light.*] Tomorrow he vill come home und admit his mistake! [*Herman appears at the window and raps with a coin.*] Dere's Hoiman vaiting out dere. Kvit cryink!

GLORY: No, Papa!

GWENDLEBAUM: He's a goot zanzible feller. Hoiman vill go a long vays in der wholesale bitzness . . . . [*He raises his voice.*] She's comink, Hoiman! [*To Glory:*] Don't led him see you ben cryink. Leo vill be all ride. Tomorrow—he vill come home und admit his mistake . . . .

[*They go out slowly. Traffic noises are heard from the street.*]

CURTAIN

## "ME, TERRY MEIGHAN, M.D.!"

*It is December 30, about eleven o'clock at night. The radio is play-ing the "Sugar Blues"\* or something similar, with Texas offering a vocal accompaniment while he and Chuck play checkers.*

*Glory stands moodily by the counter. Terry is seated in his usual corner with a newspaper spread before his face.*

GWENDLEBAUM [*entering from the office*]: Mornink noon und night, dot radio goink! Don't you know ve got a veak tube in da box? Replacements! Vun tink enudder. Over at da Fourteen Street somevun breaks a vindow. [*He looks at Texas.*] If anytink gets in my hair hit's a crooner! [*To Glory.*] Vot's da matter vit you? You don't seem to hear vot I say anymore!

GLORY: Yes?

GWENDLEBAUM [*searching his pockets*]: Vere iss my gluffs? Here. A cold night outside. Vot could Leo be doink vitout money?

TEXAS [*singing*]: "Oh, vere, oh, vere, hass my leetle dog gone!"

GWENDLEBAUM: Shot op!

[*Texas grins and makes a jump on the checkerboard.*]

TEXAS: Crown that king.

[*Chuck scratches his head.*]

GWENDLEBAUM: Vhy don't he come home I vunder?

GLORY: It wouldn't surprise me if Leo never comes home.

---

\* "Sugar Blues" was written in 1919 by Clarence Williams, jazz pianist and composer, well-known in the twenties for his many recordings.

GWENDLEBAUM: Vere could he be?

GLORY: You might have worried about that before you run him off.

GWENDLEBAUM: Me run him off!

GLORY: Yes!

GWENDLEBAUM: Don't yell at me!

GLORY: Who's yelling?

GWENDLEBAUM: I'll give you a box on your ear!

[*Glory turns sharply and goes to the window.*]

GWENDLEBAUM: No gratitude, dot's your trouble!

[*Pause. Gwendlebaum puts on his woolen reefer.*]

GLORY: Papa—

GWENDLEBAUM: Vell?

GLORY: I'm quitting this job. [*He turns, astonished.*] You'll have to get somebody else to work here.

GWENDLEBAUM: Vot?

GLORY [*almost a scream*]: Yes, I'M quitting, quitting! —I can't stand anymore of it around here.

GWENDLEBAUM: Vot's come offer you?

GLORY: It's not a girl's job and Herman—Herman don't approve of me working here. That's why he never comes in. He don't approve of it, Papa!

GWENDLEBAUM: Hoiman?!

GLORY: He wants me to get something else. Something more respectable.

GWENDLEBAUM: Hoiman? Since ven hass he been manaching my fam'ly's affairs! Led him marry you if he vants to be your boss. Ven he provides for you, den he can say vot you should or should not be doing!

GLORY: Oh, it's not just Herman.

GWENDLEBAUM: What is it, then? About Leo?

GLORY: It's myself. I'm nearly twenty, Papa. I want something—diff'rent. —I went to see Mr. Jacoby this morning.

GWENDLEBAUM: Dot kike dressmaker you mean?

GLORY: He says I can model for him—forty-five dollars a month—I could even pay board outa that.

GWENDLEBAUM: You tink I'd let you be model in dot kike's shop? Besides who'd look afder tinks here? I got my hands full at da Fourteen Street.

GLORY: Oh, you could hire somebody.

GWENDLEBAUM: And be robbed, svindled like I vas da las time! Firs Leo, den you—

GLORY: But, Papa—

GWENDLEBAUM: You do vot you please, you an Leo—Vhy should an old man like me expect any gratitude? [*He switches the radio on.*] Go on, haf your jazz! —I'm goink out to da Fourteen Street. —Maybe you bedder close up da place yourself tonight, Glory. [*He gets into his coat.*] If Leo ain't back at da flat wehn I ged home I'll phone da police! [*Still grumbling, he goes out.*]

[*Texas sings—"Nellie, the Beautiful Model"*]

GLORY: Smart!

CHUCK: You and the old man was kind of havin' it out tonight, huh?

GLORY: I'm sick of the whole business.

[*Pete and Rocky have been watching the checker game. Chuck gets up and Pete takes his place. Rocky goes to the door.*]

ROCKY: I'm goin' out.

GLORY: We close up in about half an hour.

ROCKY: That's all right. I'm spendin' the night out.

PETE: Wit Bertha? [*He and Texas laugh.*]

CHUCK: I wonder if it's gonna snow tonight.

TERRY [*looking out the window*]: No, it's clear. You can see that clock on the station tower. [*He glances at Glory.*] This is the kind of night I'd like to be going somewhere.

GLORY: Change your mind about checking out today?

TERRY [*nervously*]: Yes. I ain't quite ready. [*He moves to the stairs.*] What's this about Gwendlebaum's kid leaving home?

GLORY: He and Papa got into a fight last night.

TERRY: You're worried about him?

GLORY: Sure.

TERRY: He'll be all right. [*He goes upstairs.*]

[*She watches him. Olsen enters. He looks dazed.*]

TEXAS: Been to the hospital, Ole?

OLSEN [*in a choked whisper*]: Yes.

PETE: How's Carl?

OLSEN [*after a long pause*]: Carl's dead.

[*Texas and Pete rise.*]

GLORY: I'm sorry to hear that.

TEXAS: Come on, Ole. We'll go out and—have a drink.

[*Pete and Texas take him out.*]

GLORY [*to Chuck*]: If they come back, you let them in. I'm going.

CHUCK: Sure, I'll let 'em in. You lock up and go on home, Glory.

[*He climbs upstairs. Glory turns out all the lights except the green-shaded bulb over the counter. She is at the mirror, putting on her hat, when Abel White enters, stealthily. He strikes a match on the door edge and grins, staring at Glory. She turns quickly.*]

ABEL: Looks pretty when it burns, don't it?

GLORY [*sharply*]: I told you to stay out of here! [*Abel comes toward her.*] You want me to call the police?

ABEL [*still advancing*]: This is the way your hair would look if it caught on fire.

GLORY: Keep away with those matches! If you don't, I'll— [*She retreats to the wall, terrified.*]

ABEL: I remember you, girl. When I was in here before I saw you. I dreamed about you. I dreamed that your hair was on fire and I was—

[*His voice rises and he goes still closer. Glory screams. She darts toward the counter, Abel pursuing. Terry rushes downstairs. He grabs Abel's collar and flings him to the floor.*]

TERRY [*to Glory*]: Hurt you?

GLORY [*clasping her throat*]: No. Just scared me awful.

[*Some other men have come downstairs.*]

TERRY: Get him out of here and hand him over to the cop.

[*Abel is dragged to the door. The patrolman takes charge of him. The men go back upstairs.*]

GLORY: I guess I owe you some thanks for that.

TERRY: No. How do you expect me to sleep with a roughhouse like that going on? [*He feels his face where Abel had scratched him in the short struggle.*]

GLORY: Sure he didn't hurt you?

TERRY: No—the poor bastard.

GLORY: It looks like he scratched you. [*She touches his face with her fingers.*]

TERRY [*moving away*]: It's all right. But I could use one of them cigarettes a yours.

GLORY: Here. Keep 'em. [*She gives him the pack.*]

TERRY: Thanks. Did it scare you much? [*They light cigarettes.*]

GLORY: It was like something that happened to me a long time ago.

TERRY: Yeah?

GLORY: When I was seven or eight years old, the first night I ever come to this place, I went upstairs and an old man grabbed me and tried to pull me down on a bed—I've been scared of men ever since. All of them except Dad and Chuck and Leo and—Herman.

TERRY: The boy friend? you ain't scared of him, huh?

GLORY: No. He never gets rough.

TERRY: Don't he ever kiss you even?

GLORY [*looking at him suspiciously.*] No.

TERRY: Why not?

GLORY: I asked him not to, once.

TERRY: And he never has?

GLORY: Never since that one time.

TERRY: You didn't like it?

GLORY: NO.

TERRY: Don't you think you'd ever like being kissed by some other guy?

GLORY: No, I don't know. [*Then positively, as she senses his possible intention.*] No, of course not!

TERRY: Don't worry. I'm not gonna try.

[*She moves away. He moves directly beneath the bulb, she further toward the door.*]

GLORY [*quickly*]: You'd better not!

TERRY [*grinning*]: If you put it that way I might be tempted.

GLORY: You'd better go back upstairs. I'm closing up now.

TERRY: Wait'll I finish my cigarette. There ain't no hurry, is there?

GLORY: Not as long as you can keep your distance.

TERRY: Don't worry. I've kept my distance from plenty a good-lookin' dames. And not cause they asked me to, neither. Some of 'em would just as soon I'd come a little bit closer. Don't get the impression I'm makin' a play for you. Get that idea out of your head. Maybe I'm woman-hungry right now but I'm not the kind that grabs without bein' offered. I never had to do that.

GLORY [smiling slightly]: I'm sorry. You see, I've had some rotten times with men.

TERRY: Sure. I don't blame you for being a little cagey. I'd rather see you too much that way than the other. —Glory, you don't belong here.

GLORY: Thanks. You don't look exactly like *you* belonged here neither.

TERRY: No. I'm sort of behind the eight ball right now.

GLORY: That was my impression.

TERRY: You and me could go places.

GLORY: What do you mean?

TERRY: You know that I've got a load of hot dough on me.

GLORY: Yes. I know that.

TERRY: You don't know how I got it.

GLORY: I don't want to know.

TERRY: I don't mind telling you. You see, there's lots you don't know. Enough to fill volumes.

GLORY: What kind of volumes?

TERRY [*grinning*]: Volumes of detective stories, I guess!

GLORY: I suppose you're John Dillinger!

TERRY [*seriously*]: Dillinger's dead—I ain't.

GLORY: Who are you? What's your real name?

TERRY: You look suspicious. [*He smiles.*] You want to know my real name?— [*He moves closer and lowers his voice.*] Terry Meighan!

GLORY [*gasping*]: Terry Meighan! The man who—

TERRY: That's it.

[*There is a long pause. Glory goes to the door and opens it.*]

GLORY [*breathlessly*]: Please get out of here now. [*Terry doesn't move.*] You can't stay here any longer!

TERRY: Why not?

GLORY: I was a fool to ever let you in. And now that I know—

TERRY: I'm no diff'rent now than I was a minute ago before you knew.

GLORY: Yes, you are. Yes, you are. A minute ago you was just a nice lookin' boy an' now you're—

TERRY: Shhh! [*He smiles.*]

GLORY: Please go!

TERRY: I'm going after a while. —You ain't scared of me, are you?

GLORY: Why shouldn't I be?

TERRY: Because I'm just what I was a minute ago before you knew me. The name don't make me diff'rent except in your mind.

GLORY: I've read about Terry Meighan.

TERRY: Most everyone has. I'm famous.

GLORY: Yes. And mixed up in killings.

TERRY: Yeah, by reputation. But me, I was never no good with a gun. Me, I got sensitive fingers. Fingers that read in the dark. The others had guns. And used 'em. I read about who got shot in the next morning's papers.

GLORY: But it's still murder.

TERRY: It's not exactly murder to me. Not the way I look at it— it's more like war.

GLORY: War?

TERRY: Yes, between me an' them. Y'see. I'm a sort of one-man revolution. I haven't got any flag or ideals or stuff like that to fight for. All I've got is myself an' what I need an' what I want. I guess that sounds like a poor excuse for a guy like me to make for himself. But you can believe it or not—I only took this way cause I couldn't take any other. It's like a stone rollin' down hill. Somebody gives it a kick or shove an' off it goes, faster'n faster. It don't stop till it hits the bottom. —The bottom for me's a well-placed bullet—between the eyes or the shoulder blades. Or the end of a rope, if they ever caught me sleeping, which I don't think they will!

GLORY [*slowly, after a pause*]: I still can't believe it's true. It don't seem possible. [*Terry laughs softly.*] You being Terry Meighan, I mean.

TERRY: It scared you?

GLORY: Yes. A minute ago.

TERRY: Not now?

GLORY: Not so much now, for some reason.

TERRY: Why should it? [*He continues earnestly.*] I'm the same as anyone else underneath.

GLORY: I guess you are. What did you tell me for?

TERRY: Before I told you we was strangers. Now we ain't.

GLORY: Maybe we should've stayed strangers.

TERRY: No! We shouldn't.

GLORY: You'd better leave. It's dangerous for you to stay here.

TERRY: I don't know. They wouldn't expect to find Terry Meighan hanging out in a dump like this. I've got a reputation for taking the best accommodations where I go. But like I said, I'm down on my luck right now. That last job we pulled—cracked a bank in Detroit. I guess you read about it in the papers?

GLORY: Yes. You killed someone.

TERRY: A guard got shot. It wasn't me. There was lots of shooting.

GLORY: I don't want to hear about that part of it.

TERRY: I'm not aching to talk about it neither. We got a hundred grand on that job. But the money's too hot. None of the usual changers would take it this time, and the crowd's broke up. They killed Seibert, and Blackie was caught. Spitalni's out East trying to make some contacts. I got a message from him today in the personal column. He says for me to come on out, he's got a changer lined up. But they'll only give us thirty cents on the dollar. That ain't enough. You see, I wanta get out of this game. I don't mean feet first neither. From now on I wanta live like a regular gent!

GLORY: How could you?

TERRY: Why not?

GLORY: After killing men?

TERRY: I told you before, that ain't murder the way I look at it. It's war.

GLORY: You started it didn't you?

TERRY: No, I never started it.

GLORY: Who did start it, then?

TERRY [*fiercely*]: I'll tell you who started it. It's the ones that made a tubercular prostitute out of my mother and fixed it so's I got my education out of alleys and poolhalls and whorehouses and backstreet gambling joints instead of refined, clean places where your respectable citizens are raised.

GLORY: Now you sound like Leo!

TERRY: Maybe Leo's right. [*He takes a cigarette.*] I know what I'd have been if I ever had half a chance to be anything but what I am!

GLORY: What?

TERRY: I'd like to have been a doctor. Me, Terry Meighan, M.D. Ain't that a laugh?

GLORY: No, I'm not laughing.

TERRY: Neither am I. Here's a light. You see, I never had a chance to learn much. Barely to read and write. I had to make money somehow. God, but it made me sick to see mother go into the back room at night with men she'd picked up on the street! Hear them laughing in there! And what the kids told me they did! And then the next morning that sick grey look on her face—and her spitting up blood! —I stood as much as I could of that sort of thing and then I quit school and lammed out. I tried to go straight at first. I got me a job in a packin' house in Chicago. Bashin' hogs over the head with a club—standin' ankle deep in the muck!

GLORY [*averting her face*]: Don't!

TERRY: No, I didn't like it myself. I never felt clean. So I quit that after a while and got a job on a cattle boat. That was some better. I got a taste of real living, out there in the open, between

101

the sea and the sky. That was clean. I saw lots of swell places. Acapulco, Havana, Buenos Aires, Rio. I got an awful yen for some of them places. Travelin' around on the loose, you know, it's swell, only you got to have money to really enjoy it. Well, I decided I'd get me some coin. So I quit the boat and I went to work in a warehouse. But that way I never got nowhere. Ten dollars a week. The hell with that noise! So I quit that, too. I took half a dozen jobs and it was all the same. All I ever done was to work my tail off to make some rich guy richer. I got tired of that. See? And so I started my own little private revolution. It's been going on ever since. You've seen it in all the papers. I've crashed the headlines, Glory. When I crack a bank it's a scoop. It's big news!

GLORY: Are you proud of that? [*Pause.*]

TERRY: No, I'm pretty sick of it.

GLORY: Then why don't you stop?

TERRY: I am. I'm going East and cash in. And then I'm through.

GLORY: When you going?

TERRY: Tonight. Or tomorrow.

GLORY: Then I'll tell you—good-bye.

TERRY: No, you won't.

GLORY: Won't I? How do you mean?

TERRY: I mean that you're going with me.

GLORY: That *is* a laugh!

TERRY: You ain't laughing!

GLORY: Ain't I. I must've lost my sense of humor! What makes you think I'd go anywhere with you, even if I didn't know that you was Terry Meighan, the headline crasher?

TERRY: What makes you talk so hard?

GLORY: What've I got to be soft about!

TERRY: Didn't I just save your life or your honor or whatever it was you was fighting the firebug for?

GLORY: I thanked you for that.

TERRY: Why don't you look at me?

GLORY: Maybe I don't like to.

TERRY: Yes, you do. You told me the first night you thought I looked okay.

GLORY: I changed my mind since then.

TERRY: No, you ain't. You're scared to look at me. Not because I'm Terry Meighan but because you're a woman and you know I'm a man. You're scared that something might happen because of that.

GLORY: Shut up!

TERRY: No.

GLORY: Go on upstairs and get dressed. I thought you was clearing out.

TERRY: No. Not yet. [*He moves toward her.*]

GLORY: One fight in one night is enough.

TERRY: There ain't gonna be any fight between you and me.

GLORY: Who says there ain't?

TERRY: I do. I know. [*He takes her suddenly in his arms and kisses her violently.*]

GLORY: Don't! Let go of me! [*They struggle for a moment. She gasps and breaks away.*]

TERRY [*breathing heavily*]: There!

GLORY [*also*]: You stop!

[*Pause. Herman's solid figure is visible through the pane of glass. He raps on the window with a coin.*]

GLORY: That's—that's him!

TERRY: Who?

GLORY: Herman!

TERRY: Oh, the boy friend.

GLORY [*in a tense whisper*]: Stand back against the wall, I don't want him to see you. [*She calls.*] I'll be right out!

[*Herman turns and paces up and down beneath the outside light.*]

TERRY: What the hell do I care if he sees me?

GLORY: He'd get sore. [*Calling.*] Just a minute, Herman—I'll be right out! [*She moves to the counter, and puts on her hat at the mirror.*]

TERRY: So that's his name, is it? Herman? [*He laughs.*] It can't be true. It's too good. It suits him too perfect. Look at him, will you! He's all the Hermans in the whole universe wrapped up in one package, sealed, stamped and delivered!

GLORY [*her back to him, at the mirror*]: What's the matter with Herman?

TERRY: Nothing. I just told you I thought it was perfect.

GLORY: I don't know what you're laughing at.

TERRY: Yes, you do. I'm laughing because it's so perfect. I can appreciate anything that's perfect, so I can even appreciate a guy like Herman. You know it's guys like him that this earth was made for. It fits 'em like a glove. All the fine institutions and the laws and the ideas and the governments and everything else was made for guys like Herman. Herman's the big guy around here. He's the cock of the walk. Look at him strutting his stuff out there with a big ten-cent cigar in his mouth! He knows it's all his. It was all made for him to feel safe and comfortable in. So's he can go home an' read his newspaper an listen to his radio in perfect peace and harmony the rest of his natural life. Sure, I envy you, Herman. Me, I'm a misfit. An outcast. I got the brand of Cain on my forehead. A no-good criminal, a killer! I got to stand here flat against the wall hiding myself in the shadows so Herman won't see me. 'Cause Herman might get sore. What's the difference between me an Herman?

GLORY [*frightened*]: Shhh!

TERRY [*in a loud whisper*]: I'm bad and he's good . He keeps the laws and I don't. Why don't I? I told you why! Because I was born with two strikes against me. At least that many and maybe more.

GLORY: Please keep still!

TERRY: Maybe if my old man hadn't caught a steel rivet between the eyes when I was ten months old, I'd have turned out to be Herman. And maybe if Herman's old man hadn't been a steady worker and gotten several raises he might've turned out to be me, Terry Meighan, the public enemy. Who knows?

GLORY: Let go my arm!

TERRY: Sure. I'll let you go. Why don't you put Herman wise? You and him could turn me in for what my hide is worth. Five grand! Just think what a honeymoon you and Herman could have for yourselves on five grand! Maybe you'd rather have that than twenty-five or fifty grand with me? Cause Herman's straight and I'm crooked! Huh?

GLORY: Please let me go now!

TERRY [*releasing her*]: Go on! I think you'll come back! I'll wait here ten minutes to see if you don't!

GLORY: You'll waste your time. I'm never going to see your face again as long as I live!

[*She goes out quickly, slamming the door. Through the window we can see her take Herman's arm. They move off together. Terry comes out from the dark wall. He goes over to the door of Gwendlebaum's office—as if on an impulse—and starts to jimmy the lock. He has hardly started when Glory reappears at the door, running. Terry darts away from Gwendlebaum's office door as she comes in. They speak very fast, almost simultaneously.*]

GLORY: Terry!!

TERRY: Here! It took you less than I counted on—four minutes flat!

GLORY: I had to come back! Terry, Terry! [*She sobs and runs into his arms.*] Terry!

TERRY [*holding her*]: There now! Better?

GLORY [*sobbing*]: I had to come back!

TERRY: I knew you would.

GLORY: It was all so funny. Herman started telling me about what his boss had said to him this morning and all of a sudden I started laughing and running and Herman was shouting at the top of his voice and everything seemed to be spinning round and round so terribly fast I got dizzy. And then I was here at the door and all out of breath—I felt like—

TERRY: What?

GLORY: I had to be near you again!

TERRY: And now you are!

GLORY: Yes! —What's happened to me?

TERRY: You've just found out you're alive. [*Pause.*]

GLORY: I'm scared for you. I don't want you to stay in this place any longer, Terry. It ain't safe. I want you to go a long ways off from here.

TERRY: I will if you'll help me.

GLORY: What can I do?

TERRY: You've got the key to Gwendlebaum's office?

GLORY [*slowly*]: Yes, but—

TERRY: Then I suggest that we go inside.

GLORY: What for?

TERRY [*lightly*]: Crack Mr. Gwendlebaum's safe!

GLORY: Terry!

TERRY: Yeah? [*A long pause.*]

GLORY: It's all gone now. It's all finished. I'm going back and find Herman.

TERRY: Whadayamean?

GLORY [*bitterly*]: I thought it was *me* that you wanted!

TERRY: Sure it's you that I want. But we'll need some carfare, too, if we're gonna blow this town!

GLORY [*at the door*]: So long. I won't see you again! Ever!

TERRY [*going to restrain her*]: Glory!

GLORY [*slipping out quickly*]: So long!

CURTAIN

## "SNOW"

*New Year's Eve, about dusk. Outside the street lamps are just coming on. It is dark in the lobby except for the single light over the counter.*

*Chuck is on duty, slouched in his straight-back chair tilted against the counter. As the arc light outside the window comes on he suddenly straightens with a smothered exclamation. He leans forward, then slowly rises and creeps toward the window like a stalking cat, his eyes fixed on the area of light around the arc lamp.*

CHUCK [*under his breath*]: Snow, by Jesus, snow! [*His voice rises to a hysterical pitch of excitement.*] SNOW ! SNOW!

TEXAS [*coming downstairs*]: Yeah, I seen it before. It snowed once in Chicasaw County. Declared a bank holiday.

[*Texas rests his foot on the bench and tunes his guitar as Chuck darts frenziedly about the room, getting into his wraps and muttering to himself. Glory enters from the street.*]

CHUCK: Glory!

GLORY: Yes?

CHUCK: Look what you got on your coat sleeve. Snow. Big solid flakes. Even when you blow on it look how it stays! You think that'll melt? Naw!

GLORY: Don't get all worked up. May stop in half an hour.

CHUCK: Naw. It ain't gonna stop. I tell you it's gonna snow all night!

GLORY: I thought you had your shovel in hock?

CHUCK: Yeah! But where's Gwendlebaum?

GLORY: Stopped to get a cigar. That's him coming now.

CHUCK [*ceremoniously opening door*]: *Mist*-er Gwendlebaum!

GWENDLEBAUM [*suspiciously*]: Yas?

CHUCK: It's started to snow!

GWENDLEBAUM: Thanks for the information.

CHUCK: Listen, please!

GWENDLEBAUM: Go ahead! Vot's happened?

CHUCK [*strangled with emotion*]: I got my shovel in hock!

GWENDLEBAUM: You got your shovel in hock?

CHUCK: Yes. Understand?

GWENDLEBAUM: No. Vot does he mean? I don't understand dese slang expressions he uses! [*He turns to the counter, unwrapping his shawl.*]

CHUCK: Mr. Gwendlebaum, listen, please! I got my shovel in—

GWENDLEBAUM: Yas, you said it before—you got your shovel in hock. Vot of it? Am I responsible?

CHUCK: For six bits I could get it out!

GWENDLEBAUM: Oh. Money you vant. Now it becomes comprehensive!

CHUCK: For six bits, only six bits I could get it out and then maybe I could earn five or six dollar—understand?—five or six dollar, out in the West End shoveling off their sidewalks for 'em on New Year's Eve!

GWENDLEBAUM [*simultaneously*]: Nahhh! Go vay! You bodder me!

CHUCK [*same*]: He don't understand! He couldn't.

GLORY [*same*]: Papa, let him have it!

CHUCK: You see Mr. Gwendlebaum, they all want their walks clean for New Year's. That stand t' reason, don't it? If they don't get their walks clean it gets slippery, see? and when they come home tonight plastered after their big celebrations, what do you think they would do? Slip on the sidewalk, fall on their fannies and knock out all their brains maybe!!

GWENDLEBAUM [*cutting in*]: Go vay, I said! I got vork to do!

GLORY: Papa, now, it won't hurt you to advance him six bits on his pay?

GWENDLEBAUM: Vot pay? He sleeps here for nutting. Dot's plenty for him! I'm not running a charitable hinstitutootion!

CHUCK [*hoarsely*]: This is the chance I been waiting for. My big opportunity. It snows on New Year's Eve, the first time it done that since nineteen thirty or thirty-one! And me, I got no shovel! What do you think of that for a situation?

GWENDLEBAUM [*shortly*]: I think it's no good.

[*Texas, who has watched with amusement, begins to play a doleful blues melody on his guitar—buttons his coat and goes out.*]

GWENDLEBAUM: Turn on some lights in here! You vant people to tink we've gone out of business? [*He switches on the overhead light.*] You might as vell go on upstairs an get done vit your sveeping up dere—uddervise you can't afford to be sleeping inside tonight regardless of how much it snows or don't snow!

CHUCK: Mr. Gwendlebaum—

GWENDLEBAUM: Write a letter to Mr. President Roosevelt of the United States—tal him for God's sake to send you six bits cause you never done an honest days' vork in your life and you don't vant to do vun. Dan you vill get some quick action I promise!

CHUCK: Mr. Gwendlebaum—I'll pay you intrusht on the investment!

GLORY [*rings cash-register*]: Here's your six bits. Be careful you don't get thirsty tonight and spend it over at the Bright Spot Café.

CHUCK [*breathless with delight*]: Thanks Glory! Thanks and God bless you!

GWENDLEBAUM [*amused*]: Oh, you getting religious, are you?

CHUCK: Yes, I'm getting religious, Mr. Gwendlebaum. You know when it snows and a man's got a shovel it makes him even believe in God! [*In his haste to get out he bumps into Jabe who is entering.*]

JABE: Watch where you're going, screwball!

CHUCK: Excuse me. [*He scurries out. Jabe goes upstairs.*]

GWENDLEBAUM [*to Glory*]: You're too easy vit them. Now he'll go out and get drunk and come back here begging for anudder six bits—'advance on his pay!'—No sign of Leo. Vot clothes did he have on ven he left?

GLORY: You saw him as well as I did.

GWENDLEBAUM: No. I vas too upset. He had on his overcoat, No?

GLORY: He had an overcoat.

GWENDLEBAUM: He vouldn't stay out again tonight, vould he, you tink?

GLORY: I'm tired of thinking. You'll have to think for yourself.

GWENDLEBAUM: Nah. He'll come home. Or do you think I should notify der police to get out a search for him?

GLORY: I think that Leo will come home. He isn't the kind to do anything—terribly—drastic.

GWENDLEBAUM: Drastic? Vot could be more—drastic—dan get-tink himself kicked out from da collich.

GLORY: That's just kid stuff. He'll get over that. In a day or two he'll come home and go back to school. Some day he'll be tellng some other fresh punk to take his choice between getting a college degree or reforming the world.

GWENDLEBAUM [*suspiciously*]: Vere do you get dot stuff from?

GLORY [*absently*]: Nowhere.

GWENDLEBAUM: He's got his modder's constitution. Vould be like him to catch lung trouble an' go like she done.

GLORY: He's thin, but he's got resistance.

GWENDLEBAUM: Resistance of da wrong kind. Vere's all our distinguished patrons?

GLORY: It's New Year's. They'll be out late.

GWENDLEBAUM: Vit Chuck gone out you'll have to stay.

GLORY: All right.

GWENDLEBAUM: Vot's become of da smart-dressed fellow dot sits around all da time vit a newspaper up in front of his face?

GLORY: He's gone.

GWENDLEBAUM: Checked out? Did he pay?

GLORY: Yes.

GWENDLEBAUM: I had my suspicous. He looked like a *gonif.*[*]

GLORY: He was okay.

GWENDLEBAUM: I had an idea that maybe you thought he was. Fellows like him don't belong around here and they ain't around

---

[*] *Gonif*— Hebrew for 'thief' or 'rascal'.

here for no good. —I been thinking. Maybe you're right about getting a job some place else. If Hoiman ain't serious in his attentions maybe you better get started at some udder thing.

GLORY: Oh, I don't know.

GWENDLEBAUM: Hoiman's a good steady feller. But you ain't— sweet on him?

GLORY: I don't know, Papa.

GWENDLEBAUM: He's not the type like you see in the movies, but Hoiman vill go a long vay in da wholesale business.

GLORY: Yes, it's guys like Herman the world was made for!

GWENDLEBAUM: What?

GLORY: Nothing.

GWENDLEBAUM: You been needing a change. Maybe a little trip someveres vould do you some good. Soon as Leo comes back ve'll make some kind of arranchment— Good night. [*He goes out.*]

[*Glory goes to the counter. Terry slips in quietly. He has on a smart new overcoat, hat, gloves. His shoes are glittering. He seats himself in his usual corner and unfolds his newspaper before his face. Glory turns sharply and sees him. She stares at him for a moment. Then she comes from behind the counter and switches off the overhead light.*]

GLORY: Terry!

TERRY: Yes, it's me.

GLORY: I thought you was gone.

TERRY: So did I.

GLORY: What did you come back for?

TERRY: I forgot something.

GLORY: What?

TERRY: You.

GLORY [*voice hardening*]: We settled all that last night.

TERRY: Nothing was settled last night.

GLORY: It wasn't me that you wanted.

TERRY: It was.

GLORY: You wanted the money from Papa's safe.

TERRY: I wanted money enough to get us both outa town, that was all. Didn't wanta run the risk of blowin' them hot centuries of mine around here. We needed carfare, didn't we? That's the only way I knew of to get it!

GLORY: You wanted to use me.

TERRY: You know that's a lie.

GLORY: I know it's the truth.

TERRY: What do you think I come back here for tonight if it wasn't because I had to have you? I couldn't leave here without you.

GLORY: You're leaving without me. I ain't going nowhere with you. I don't want your kind of life and I don't want any part of it. Can't you get that through your head?

TERRY: No.

GLORY: You must have a pretty thick skull. But it ain't bullet-proof. You hang around here much longer you'll find that out. I seen Jabe talking to a plainclothes man and even Papa called you a *gonif* just now. If he comes back in here and sees you sittin' here dressed like that he'll call the police sure!

TERRY: I should think you'd call 'em yourself. Tell 'em you've captured Terry Meighan, fugitive from Justice, an' collect your five grand.

GLORY: I don't want that kind of money. Where did you get those clothes you got on?

TERRY [*turning proudly*]: Good-lookin' front? Got a complete new outfit even to gloves. I like gloves. [*He pulls them off tenderly.*] Makes me feel like a gentleman wearin' kid gloves.

GLORY: How did you get all that?

TERRY: Bought 'em.

GLORY: What with?

TERRY: I didn't crack your Papa's safe.

GLORY: No. You cracked those yellow-back bills.

TERRY: Sure.

GLORY: You fool! Get out of here quick!

TERRY: You're going with me.

GLORY: You think I want to get shot full of holes? No, thanks. How long do you think it'll take 'em to trace that money?

TERRY: Even if the dough's still hot we got plenty of time. This here's New Year's Eve. Nobody does nothing on New Year's Eve but get drunk. And blow whistles. And have a swell time. And you and me, we'll celebrate, too. Hundred dollars are flyin' around this city like pigeons tonight. Nobody even looks at 'em. And by the time they do, we'll be gone, you an' me. Look out that window. See that neat job over there? No you can't, it's snowing too thick—but it's one of them Packard Sixes. Only got 800 miles on it. Picked it up for a song. And is she a stepper? You know it! Know where we're going? Acapulco! It's a place down in Mexico where they got water the same shade as your eyes! Yeah. You like the idea, don't you? Tonight we'll celebrate. A little private celebration. We don't need to go to any of them fancy places. I know a place round the corner. They don't ask questions. They're deaf, dumb and blind like the monkeys!

GLORY: What do you mean?

TERRY: Glory—what are you scared of? We'll be 'cross the Mexican border before the P.D.'s had time to sleep off their hangovers!

GLORY: It's you I'm scared of.

TERRY: Me? I'll take care of you!

GLORY: Yes, you'd give me lots of protection. You'd stand in between me and the machine guns when the cops start firing.

TERRY: Sure I would. I wouldn't let nothing hurt you as long as I had a breath in my body.

GLORY: You wouldn't have long. They're likely to come here after you any minute. What do you think that officer was talkin' to Jabe about?

TERRY: That's Jabe's business, talkin' to cops. He's got nothing on me. Besides we're practically gone.

GLORY: You're wasting your breath. I won't go.

[*She turns and goes to the window. The Cathedral bells begin chiming the hour.*]

Listen to them cathedral bells ringing.

TERRY: What about 'em?

GLORY: I never heard 'em ring like that before.

TERRY: They sound the same as always to me.

GLORY: No, they sound diff'rent. They sound like they knew something that I don't know. —It's no use fighting against what's going to happen. [*She turns to him.*] It's like you said. There's something between you an' me. I don't know what. I didn't go back to Herman last night. I couldn't. I ran home and stuffed my head in a pillow and cried till morning. Oh, God, how I prayed for you, Terry—but somehow I known that it wouldn't do you no good or me either.

TERRY: Glory! [*He pulls her against him.*]

GLORY: You wasn't lying when you said you'd take care of me?

TERRY: I wasn't lying.

GLORY: I believe you. I can't believe nothing else when I look at your face. I want to look at your face a long time in the light where I can see it real plain. When I look at your face in the light I can almost forget there was ever anything ugly on earth. I can't look at Herman's face like that. When I look at him I just think of—neat little pen-scratches across a piece of white paper. Columns of figures to add or subtract or divide. Maybe that's clean, too. But it ain't the kind of cleanness that you've got, Terry. You've got the cleanness of big things in you. Know what I mean? Mountains and rivers an oceans an things of that kind. That's why when Herman started talking about what he said to the boss and the boss said to him, I started laughing and couldn't stop and come running back here out of breath cause I had to be near you again. And when you asked me to unlock Papa's office for you so you could crack the safe open— It was like the whole sky had come crashing down on my head— Promise me, Terry, there won't be nothing like that from now on.

TERRY: I give you my word on that. Listen how quiet it is now. The bells've stopped ringing. It's so quiet you can almost hear the snow fall. It makes a sound like cat's feet walking on velvet. Even softer than that. It makes a sound like your breath does coming in and out of your body. There's nothing softer than that. There's nothing any sweeter than that is, Glory. What've you got to be scared of? Nothing. Look out there and see for yourself. There's nothing out there but snow. Nobody, nothing but snow. And look how thick it's falling. You can't hardly see the cathedral. And them big buildings, them places that guys like your Herman go in every morning and come out of at night, they're all gone, disappeared, there ain't a sign of 'em left—the Telephone building, the Western-Pacific, the Union Light and Power! Them big places that the clock-punchers belong to, that own 'em body 'an soul—they ain't got nothing on us, not any part of us, Glory! They just ain't there any more. Maybe they never was there. I heard a guy on a street corner. Soapbox speaker. Pointed up at them buildings. Said some day we was gonna tear 'em down, we was gonna stamp 'em into the dust. Won't be any more big corporations, he said, no more financial octopuses enslavin' the masses, we'll tear 'em all down, he says, an' grind 'em into the dust. We'll have us a revolution, he says, an' the people will own it all, they'll be on the top. Won't have to punch clocks no more for the bosses, they'll live an' breathe an' walk alive in the sun like human bein's. [*He turns back from the window to Glory.*] It was a good speech all right. Made me feel hot all over. And then I laughed and I said to myself, 'You tell 'em, buddy, some day there'll be pie in the sky for all comers! I'll take mine now, I said to myself, I won't wait for the angels to start dishing it out on gold platters!' An so I bought me a sawed-off shotgun at a second-hand store and stuck up the guy that sold it to me the very next night. That was my kind of salvation. Hell, I didn't want to wait for social justice like the guy called it, I thought I'd take mine now and avoid the crowds!

GLORY: Don't talk like that!

TERRY: Why not?

GLORY: It ain't right.

TERRY: I know. That's all past now. I'm a criminal, killer, outlaw — because I wanted to live and didn't find no other way! But that's all past. That snow out there's like a curtain come down on all that. We've gotten away from 'em, Glory. They'll never catch up with us now. We're fugitives all right. —But not from *justice*. We never *had* any justice!

GLORY: Terry!

TERRY: Yeah [*He laughs.*] First time in my life I ever busted loose with so many words. Let's go!

GLORY: Where?

TERRY: That place round the corner—you don't have to sign a book even—just lay down your money an' go upstairs!

GLORY: I couldn't do that. I couldn't.

TERRY: No?

GLORY: Not without I was— !

TERRY: Married? [*He laughs.*] We got lots of time for that later. Right now we don't want preachers an' people askin' us questions, makin' us write things down! —Honey, we've had this boiling in us too long to be put off any more! Glory— [*He kisses her hungrily.*]

GLORY: Couldn't we wait till—

TERRY: You don't wanta wait an' me neither. We're gonna be drivin' straight through twenty-four hours with no stop-offs anywhere between here an' the border except to fill the tank up! — Tonight's New Year's Eve. We can take three hours together— Then come back here an' leave a note for Gwendlebaum so he won't get suspicious an' set the cops on our tails!

GLORY: I got to think first, I've got to *think*, Terry!

TERRY: No!

GLORY: I've got some things here—

TERRY: We'll pick 'em up later! Come on!

GLORY: It's going so fast! [*She catches her head in her hands.*]

TERRY: What is?

GLORY: The world! I can feel it turning. It's going a thousand miles a minute! [*She laughs a little wildly.*]

TERRY: You bet it is! And we're going with it— Come on! Come on!

[*Laughing, he flings the door open. They slip out together and their shadows fly across the big window and are gone—*]

SLOW CURTAIN

# SCENE SEVEN

## "THE BIG CELEBRATION"

*In this scene the play veers sharply upward in its progression from the realistic to the lyrical plane. This change should be accomplished as smoothly as possible so that the audience will not have a sense of distortion. The stage will be lightless except for the arc lamp beyond the large window, and the effects of the room, the benches, counter, etc., will be so nearly indistinguishable that the setting might almost be that of a cathedral. Chuck's speeches will remain upon the realistic plane but Leo's will really be passages of poetry and will have to be delivered as such. The lyrical atmosphere will continue into the final scene and must be carefully built-up and a collapse into melodrama must be skillfully avoided by the actors.*

*As the curtain rises Leo is discovered seated on a bench by the window. His identity, of course, is not known till he speaks. Chuck enters the outside door, drunkenly.*]

CHUCK: Who's that over there.

LEO: It's me, Chuck.

CHUCK [*peering*]: Who?

LEO: Me, Leo.

CHUCK: Oh. Christamighty, boy, they told me you'd run away.

LEO: I tried to but I couldn't. I didn't have the guts to stick it out.

CHUCK: Huh?

LEO: It was too big for me. Too damn big. I couldn't buck up against it.

CHUCK: Whadayamean was too big?

LEO: The city out there.

CHUCK: Big? This town? [*With disgust.*] Ahh, you oughta see Chicago.

LEO: They're all too big. Look at them, those towers out there. Twenty, thirty stories. What chance has one man got against all that?

CHUCK: Drunk, aintcha?

LEO: Drunk? No.

CHUCK: Whatsamatter with ya then? Yuh talkin' kind of onnatcheral.

LEO: I don't feel natural. I haven't had a bite to eat in three days.

CHUCK: Tree days witout eatin'? No wonder yuh gone off yer nut! Better go on home, kid'n, git some food'n sleep.

LEO: I don't want food'n sleep. I want to see Glory. Where is she?

CHUCK: She oughta been here. The old man left her in charge.

LEO: She wasn't here when I came.

CHUCK: What time's it now? Can't see. Let's have some light in this place [*He moves toward the light.*]

LEO [*sharply*]: No, leave it off! —I like it dark.

CHUCK: Okay. I just wanta see what the time is. [*He strikes a match.*] Goin' on twelve. Glory shouldena closed up yet. I reckon it bein' New Year's Eve they've all of gone out places so she went out, too.

LEO: I've got to talk to her.

CHUCK: What about?

LEO: I was desperate, I—I started to jump off the bridge.

CHUCK [*incredulous*]: Naw!

LEO: It was Glory that stopped me.

CHUCK: Glory was out there on the bridge?

LEO: No, but it seemed like she was. I heard her voice saying 'Leo!' just as I started to hoist myself over the rail and I turned around and bumped right into a cop and he said, 'What the hell are you doing out here?' I said, 'Watching the river, that's all.' He said, 'The river don't need any watching. It won't run away!' I said, 'Yes, it does. It's running away as fast as it can and I'll be damned if I blame it. Who wouldn't want to be running away from this lousy town?' And that got him sore and he gave me a poke with his billy and said, 'Move on, buddy, keep moving!' — And I just laughed in his face. I said, 'Thank you, copper. That's the best advice you ever gave anyone yet—keep moving!' —He looked at me like he thought I was crazy. I guess he was right. There was only one thought in my head that I can remember and that was to get back here as fast as I can and see Glory before I changed my mind again and decided to run on off with the river!

CHUCK: Huh! I guess you'd better see Glory if you got any ideas like that in yer head. Why dontcha go on home now? Maybe you'll find Glory there.

LEO: I can't go home.

CHUCK: Why cantcha?

LEO: I'm ashamed to. I couldn't face Papa again.

CHUCK: What's all this about anyhow? Y'got kicked outa school, huh?

LEO: I don't know what got into me. I lost my head.

CHUCK: What didja do?

LEO: You saw it. That holiday paper we published.

CHUCK: Oh, that stuff you wrote against the army. I warned you.

LEO: It wasn't just that. I'd written a lot of other things. And said things. And so they took away my scholarship. Papa wanted me to write 'em a letter of apology, take back all I'd said, beg 'em to let me back in. That would've been the smart thing to do, but I'm not smart—I couldn't do it.

CHUCK: Sure yuh could if yuh tried.

LEO: Oh, I suppose I'll have to now. —I'm licked. It was too big out there. Too many streets, too many people. I got all confused. It didn't look that way from the streetcars when I was going to school in the mornings. It looked like I belonged to it then. The people's faces looked like mine and they seemed to be doing the kind of things that I could be doing. But that was all a mistake, an optical illusion. I found that out when I tried to get out there and be like they were. —I didn't belong.

CHUCK [*passing bottle*]: Have one.

LEO: Thanks, Chuck. [*He takes swallow.*] That's my first drink of whiskey. [*Shuddering.*] Mmmm!

CHUCK: How does it taste to yuh?

LEO: Is that what people put inside themselves to have a good time?

CHUCK: Just wait. One swallow don't make a summer. I'll admit that this here ain't the best obtainable at any price. [*He drinks.*] Ugh! But it sure hits the spot. Me, I'm drunk. You wanta know why?

LEO: People get drunk so they can hide from the truth about things!

CHUCK: Yeah. Me I got drunk so's I wouldn't have t' think about my shovel being in hock and me not having the money t' git it out. And all that snow comin down out there, just a-beggin t' be scraped off. I tell yuh I coulda gone stark ravin' mad just thinkin about it. But now I feel good. [*He drinks again.*] Yes, sir, I feel pretty good.

[*Jabe enters cautiously, apparently unaware of anyone's presence. He goes to the counter and dials the phone.*]

JABE: Gimme Mr. O'Connor. [*Pause.*] Hello, Mr. O'Connor? She ain't here. Naw, that's right. Him and her together, musta been about tree owrs ago in a Packard six, and they ain't got back yet. Sure he'll bring her back, she's got to close up; that is, unless they've already blown outa town. But you can pick 'em up easy in a bus like that. Sure. Y'know me. I'd say in about ha'f'n owr. — [*He hangs up and goes out quickly.*]

CHUCK: Shounds like that dirty rat was puttin' the finger on shomebody, don't it? [*There is a slight pause to emphasize the ominous note of the next speech.*]

LEO [*to himself*]: Death's like the river.

CHUCK: What's that?

LEO: I said that death's like the river. It's dark and running away. —But Glory, she's a woman.

CHUCK: Oh. Glory's a woman all right. A damn good one. It was her that give me that six bits I had t' git my shovel outa hock with. [*Bitterly.*] Yeah, but they wanted to charge a dollar forty-five cents. It sheems like the intrush had mounted up t' more'n I figgered on somehow. I told 'em t' keep th' goddam thing. So instead a my shovel I got m'self whiskey t' drink. Have another.

LEO [*drinking*]: Thanks.

CHUCK: Take a good one. Forget your troubles, like me. [*He turns on the radio. There is a blare of merrymaking— "There'll be a Hot Time in the Old Town Tonight."*] Lissen to them rich bastards having their big celebration. [*He switches off the radio.*] I guess they musta got somebody else t' scrape off their sidewalks tonight. [*For Chuck this is profound tragedy: then he speaks with bravado.*] Well, what do I care? I'm havin' a good time, ain't I? — Well, AIN'T I? [*He is almost pleading.*]

LEO: Yes, a good time—

CHUCK: You bet! I'm havin' a WONDERFUL time! — [*His false bravado collapses: his whole figure sags.*] —Only I wish I hadn't gotten so thirsty last summer . . . . Just look at it falling out there!

LEO: Yes, the snow's beautiful at night. [*Then softly.*] It gives you an illusion of escape . . . .

CHUCK [*wobbling toward the window*]: Shtill as thick as ever!

LEO: It's covering up the whole city.

CHUCK: I'd say it was three inches deep! Maybe four!

LEO: All you can see is the snow.

[*He walks slowly toward the window till his figure is silhouetted against its light. His movements must prepare the audience for the lyrical speech to follow. During the pause, Chuck's figure sags on the bench.*]

Those buildings aren't there anymore. You can't see the Union Light and Power. The Cosmopolitan Trust has disappeared. The Western Pacific's been blotted out by the snow. —Tonight's God's night of sleep, I suppose. He's tired of looking at the nasty mess we've made of ourselves. He's pulled down a big white shade to cover us up. Now our stink can't reach his nostrils. Our squawling's drowned in the long white feathery thunder of snow. . . . [*With rising bitterness.*] But he's got the alarm clock set for half-past seven. And in the morning it will all get started again. [*With savage irony.*] Bombs will explode in the streets of Shanghai, and the rebels will make another drive on the lines at Barcelona. Russia will write a note of protest to Japan. Italy will issue a warning. Germany will take a firm stand. There will be aerial maneuvers in southern France and the British fleets will be concentrated at strategic points along the Mediterranean. A sailor who's guided a wheel by the stars will have both eyes blown out. Some girl's letter to her lover will be illegibly blurred with blood from a wound in his heart. And in this city a man will go mad with paresis, another with terror, a third will drown himself and the newspapers will report death from cancer and cerebral hemorrhage among our leading citizens, and there will be casual mention of various epidemics, of lust murders, of famine and starvation, and the decline of Utilities on the New York Exchange. But all that's forgotten tonight, God's asleep. And if you have any questions to ask about the chaotic conditions on this little spherical toy of his, you'll have to refer them to his secretary, who will send you form letter No. X99 explaining that accidents will happen and that of course God's ways are necessarily rather obscure to man . . . . [*He sinks slowly onto the bench.*]

CHUCK [*after a moment*]: How do you feel?

LEO: Warm inside.

CHUCK: It's hittin' you pretty quick not havin' no food on yuh belly.

LEO: I feel it already.

CHUCK: Sure, it's like eating raw meat. —[*Then eagerly.*] If I had halfa dollar left outa that money I'd go around and see Bertha! — Y'know Bertha?

LEO: No.

CHUCK: Bertha's a snowbird, but hell, I seen a lot worse'n she is. She's round the corner at the Ritz Hotel. Like to go?

LEO: No.

CHUCK: Maybe some other time, huh?

LEO: No.

CHUCK: I bet you never been out wit a girl like Bertha.

LEO: No. I don't want to.

CHUCK: That's what's wrong with you. Only yuh don't know it. Guys like you, you young punks that wanta make the world over, what's really wrong with you is you ain't found out why they put two pillows on one bed. Berth'd put you wise.

LEO: I guess there's lots of things I'll have to find out.

CHUCK: Things they don't teach at college.

LEO: What's wrong with me, Chuck? Why don't I belong out there with the rest of those people? I've tried to pretend like I did. I went in those places where they work and I tried to ask for a job. But I couldn't.

CHUCK: Naw?

LEO: The words got stuck in my mouth. It scared me to watch them doing those things they were doing, operating machines, writing figures, selling goods, bustling around with piles and piles of letters and orders and—business! That's the whole thing to them and to me it's nothing at all. It doesn't exist, it's a world that I don't belong to, full of strangers. The only thing that I'm any good for, Chuck, is putting words down on paper. And what's the use of that? [He rises.] Do you know what's wrong with that city out there?

CHUCK: Naw. What?

LEO: It got too big for the people that built it, it doesn't belong to them any more—they belong to it!

CHUCK: Huh?

LEO: They built themselves a big trap to jump into. Like the man that was building a house—did you hear about him?

CHUCK: Naw.

LEO: He stood on the inside and built the house all around him, on all four sides of him—see? but he forgot to make any doors or any windows—so when it was finished, the man, he couldn't get out!

CHUCK: Yeh? [*He takes a drink.*]

LEO: Yeh, they're all caught in it except just a few like us, you an' me, the poor bums that flop here— Us, we didn't build walls around us, we don't belong— No, we're outcasts, lunatics, criminals—the Fugitive Kind, that's what we are—the ones that don't wanta stay put.

[*Cathedral bells begin ringing. At this signal a sound of celebration commences. Horns are blown, tin cans rattle, firecrackers explode.*]

LEO [*to window*]: Listen to 'em!

CHUCK: Yeah!

LEO: Toot-toot! Blah-blah! They're havin' a big celebration!

[*People rush past the window in a Carnival spirit, wearing paper hats and blowing tin horns. "Hail, Hail, the gang's all here!"*]

LEO: But they can't keep it up very long.

[*The sounds of revelry fade—the cathedral bells go on ringing.*]

LEO: They're quieting down now. Now all you can hear is just the cathedral bells ringing. You know what that is? That's the voice inside of 'em saying it's all no use, it's no good. Did you ever hear anything so awful an' sad as that is? God, I wonder if they hear it, too! Or is it just inside of me those bells are ringin' like that? Huh, Chuck?

[*Pause. The ringing dies out softly.*]

LEO: I'm tired . . . .

CHUCK [*slumped on bench*]: You don't wanta go with me, huh? [*Pause.*] To Bertha's? Bertha would like you, kid. Are yuh broke? Aintcha got half a dollar? Huh? Lissen, Bertha likes joolry, too. If you give her that little ring you got on your finger I bet it would be okay. Lemme see that ring, Leo just a minute.

[*He pulls off Leo's ring—Leo has sunk down on a bench in drunken, exhausted sleep.*]

CHUCK: That's a nice ring. Is it gold? Silver? Hell, I can't see in this light. [*He goes to the door and holds the ring to the arc light.*] I bet it's your school ring, ain't it? Hey! Leo! [*More softly.*] Leo? Are you asleep? [*Then exultantly in a whisper.*] Yeah! I'll just be gone for a minute, I'm goin' round to see Bertha, I'll be right back— !

[*He opens the door—singing is heard: "Hail, hail, etc." —It fades as the merrymakers move on. Chuck slips out the door.*]

DIM OUT AND SLOW CURTAIN

# SCENE EIGHT

## "THEY WON'T EVER CATCH OUR KIND"

*Between this and the preceding scene the stage may be darkened momentarily to indicate a passage of time—or the scene may follow directly if the producer prefers. The stage is very quiet, very dark, only the arc light shining through the door and the faint electric glow of the city outlining its towers through the big window upstage.*

*Leo sleeps on a bench but cannot be seen in the dark. After a few moments the outside door opens softly. Glory slips in, followed by Terry.*

GLORY: Terry, we shouldn't have come back here.

TERRY: We won't be long. All you gotta do's write a little note to Papa Gwendlebaum to keep him from getting suspicious. We don't want him setting the cops on us, honey.

GLORY: No, but what shall I say?

TERRY: Anything! Just let him know you gone cause you wanted to go. Violating the Mann Act's* one thing I ain't been charged with yet. Got a pencil?

GLORY: There one on the desk. Wait. I'll turn the light on.

TERRY: Naw, leave it off, we don't need no lights in here.

GLORY: Oh, I forgot.

TERRY: What?

GLORY: We're the kind that has to hide in the dark, ain't we, Terry? I can't get used to that. I've always been scared of the

---

* The Mann Act— An act of Congress in 1910 prohibiting transportation of women across state lines for immoral purposes

dark and wanted the light and now it's the other way round . . . .

TERRY: Down there it won't be like that.

GLORY: Down where?

TERRY: At Acapulco!

GLORY: At Aca—pulco! It's got such a crazy sound to it—I still can't believe it's real.

TERRY: Shhh! —Quit bangin' them drawers.

GLORY: Oh, yes, we've got to be quiet, don't we? We're—we're *fugitives*! That word scares me a little!

TERRY [*laughing but a little impatient*]: Come on, come on, quit fooling! What've you got in them boxes?

GLORY: A few little things of mine—compact, comb and brush an' stuff. Look!

TERRY: What?

GLORY: Leo give me this for Xmas! —It's a manicure set! Ain't it swell?

TERRY: Honey, I can buy you all the junk like that you want! Hurry on—we gotta be gone from here.

GLORY: Naw, tell me! What's it really like? That place we're goin' to? Is it nice an' clean, Terry?

TERRY: Yeh, clean's how it is! Everything down there looks like it's just been shipped from the factory, f.o.b.

GLORY: Yeah?

TERRY: Even the stars have got that bran' new shine to 'em like they was laid out on a counter for people to buy in a jewelry store or something. Why, they're so close at night you feel like if you just reached up your hand a little bit higher you could brush the tips of 'em with the tips of your fingers! Lissen! We'll get us a room with a skylight up in the ceiling so we can lay on our backs an' look up an' imagine we're floatin' aroun' in the sky—

GLORY: I don't need lookin' through skylights to feel that way when I'm layin' beside you, Terry!

TERRY: Honey, you love me?

GLORY: Don't—don't *ask* me! It would take too long for me to tell! Oh, Terry, if I only wasn't so scared of what's going to happen maybe!

TERRY: Nothing's going to happen.

GLORY: Those cathedral bells scared me so. They had such a—such an awful *blue* sound, like I'd never heard 'em before, as though they was cryin' or somethin' or tellin' me things would go wrong!

TERRY [*nervously*]: Get that note written.

GLORY: Yes, Terry.

TERRY: And then we'll be gone. You know what the word gone means?

GLORY: I got a gone feeling right now.

TERRY: That ain't what it means. It's that feeling you get when the gats quit barkin' behind you like dogs on the chase, not hearing them bastards no more whizzing past you, the whine of 'em stingin' your ears—an inch out of death! And the town dropping back, the houses an' walls scattered out. And the first clean patch of the sky with a sprinkle of stars like cold water dashed in your face when you're half dead of thirst—that's what gone means! — It means you've gotten away and you thank God for it— Because you believe in God then—yes, in spite of the fact that you're on the wrong side and you know that God's gotta be on the right. You thank him just the same because you're alive and you can't help thinking that he's responsible for it somehow. The cops ain't got you. And there's the wind in your face and eight good cylinders humming under your feet on the boards. And you smell the woods all at once. Or an open field. You turn down a new road. A concrete slab that slides under the wheels like silk. Your back straightens up. You let the kink out of your spine and your hair flattens down to the wind, you settle back in the seat and relax and you let the car go riding straight out as clean as a knife down the road —Not being afraid no more, not being shot at. You know that you've gotten away, out of sight, out of reach! [*His voice drops.*] You see? That's what it means to be gone!

GLORY [*after a slight pause*]: I don't know as I could feel that way about it. I couldn't get much kick out of being gone if it just means out of the range of a bullet.

TERRY: Hell, you've got as much to get away from as I have. Workin' in a flophouse, goin' out with a sap named Herman whose only line of conversation is what he said to his boss and his boss said to him—you're gettin' away from all that— Fugitives from justice? Naw, we're fugitives from *in*-justice, honey! We're runnin' away from stinkin' traps that people tried to catch us in! Now, honey, get that stuff wrapped up and— *Wait!*

[*He catches her arm and pulls her back in the shadows—*
*O'Connor passes in front of the window, pauses to light a cig-*
*arette and glances inside. Terry and Glory flatten themselves*
*against the wall to avoid the light through the window.*]

TERRY [*in a whisper*]: Who's that out there?

GLORY: I don't know. I'm not sure. —But it looks like Mr.
O'Connor!

TERRY: O'Connor? Who's he?

GLORY: A friend of Jabe's.

TERRY: Jabe's? Christ, we've got to get out of this place!

GLORY [*terrified*]: You think— !

TERRY: I don't know. There must be a back way out.

GLORY: The fire escape from the dormitory.

TERRY: You better go out the front way so he'll think you're
alone and I'll go out the back.

GLORY: No, don't leave me. He might ask questions.

TERRY: You stayed down late on account of it's New Year's—
that's all. D'you see?

GLORY: Yes. But don't leave me.

TERRY: Come on, hold on to yourself! —He's gone now. He's
crossed the street— Look, he's gone into the Bright Spot Café.
Maybe it wasn't O'Connor at all. You might be mistaken, huh?

GLORY: I don't know, Terry.

[*The cathedral bells toll.*]

GLORY: It's those bells again! They scare me!

TERRY: They're ringin' for three o'clock, honey. Now— It's all okay now! Are you ready?

GLORY: Yes.

[*They move toward the door. Leo stirs on the bench and calls in his sleep.*]

LEO: Glory . . . .

GLORY [*sharply*]: Who's that?

TERRY: Huh! It's just an old drunk passed out!

LEO: Glory!

GLORY [*darting toward him*]: It's Leo! It's *Leo! He's come back!*

TERRY: Leave him be—we ain't got time.

GLORY [*bending over him*]: Leo, what's the matter? Something's happened to Leo! He's hurt or something!

TERRY: Glory, we ain't got time! Are you crazy?

GLORY: He's sick I tell you!

TERRY: Aw, he's drunk—passed out, that's all. I'll put him on a bed upstairs an' go out the back way—you meet me in the car and for God's sake, hurry!

[*He raises Leo and supports him toward the stairs. Leo mumbles drunkenly.*]

TERRY: Come along, Comrade—the revolution's over!

GLORY: Be careful with him! Be sure you cover him up!

[*Terry carries Leo upstairs. Glory goes to the counter and turns on the green-shaded bulb for a moment—then she gasps aloud, remembering the danger. Turns the light off and hastily closes box containing a few little articles she removed from the desk. Then O'Connor reappears outside the window. He carries a flashlight: its beam is directed through the window and across the floor.*]

GLORY [*rushing to the stairs and calls breathlessly*]: Terry—
TERRY!

[*O'Connor opens the door and comes inside. He turns the flashlight full upon Glory's face as she stands at the foot of the stairs, frozen with panic.*]

GLORY: Oh!

O'CONNOR: Hello.

GLORY [*breathlessly*]: What do you want?

O'CONNOR: Oh, I'm just making a little routine investigation—
Going upstairs?

GLORY: No.

O'CONNOR [*with a casual air*]: That's good. I wouldn't advise you to. —I was sure surprised when you turned on the light just now and I saw you in here. [*He comes slowly forward, watchfully, as he speaks.*]

GLORY [*as though hypnotized*]: Yes.

O'CONNOR: Work here, don't you?

GLORY: Yes.

O'CONNOR: I thought I'd seen you before. Gwendlebaum's daughter?

GLORY: Yes.

O'CONNOR: You're opening up pretty early. [*He glances at his watch.*] I got just about three o'clock.

GLORY: Yes.

O'CONNOR: Don't usually open up this early, do you?

[*Car brakes are heard outside.*]

GLORY [*her voice nearly failing*]: No—not—usually.

[*Several men appear at the window. Glory stares at them in helpless panic.*]

O'CONNOR: What's the matter?

GLORY: Nothing.

O'CONNOR: You look nervous.

[*The men enter.*]

GLORY [*almost screaming*]: What do you want?

O'CONNOR [*sharply*]: Upstairs!

GLORY: *TERRY!*

[*Her cry is like a burst of flame, exploding the charged atmosphere of the scene. O'Connor jumps forward and grasps her wrists as the men charge the chairs. She fights frantically to break loose.*]

O'CONNOR: Stuck on him, were you?

GLORY: Let go of me! Oh, for God's sake, let me go, let me go!

O'CONNOR: Take it easy!

GLORY: There's only the men upstairs! The men sleeping! Nobody else I swear!

[*Sudden shouting is heard above and the noise of pursuit.*]

O'CONNOR: There ain't?

GLORY: Let go of me, you! Why don't you let go? [*She sobs wildly.*]

[*A burst of gunfire is heard.*]

GLORY [*screaming*]: *TERRY!*

[*Shouting and running footsteps above.*]

GLORY: TERRY! TERRY! [*She falls to her knees, sobbing and struggling to free herself from O'Connor's grasp.*]

O'CONNOR: Easy there!

GLORY: What are they killing him for? What for, oh, what for? He wanted to get away, only to get away, only to get away, that was all, a thousand miles off from this place! Let us go, Oh, my God, Mister, *please* let us go!!

[*More gunfire is heard upstairs, then shouting, and running footsteps on stairs.*]

VOICE [*above*]: Stop him, O'Connor! He's comin' down front!

[*O'Connor catches Glory and holds her in front of him as he faces the stairs—Terry suddenly appears, crouching, wild-eyed, with drawn revolver.*]

TERRY [*on landing*]: Stand out from behind that girl, God damn you!

O'CONNOR: Drop your gun!

TERRY: Naw! [*He advances.*] Stand out from behind the girl!

GLORY: Terry, he'll kill you!

[*Men charge downstairs behind Terry. As he wheels to face them O'Connor opens fire at his back. The gun drops from Terry's fingers and he sags forward.*]

OFFICER ON STAIRS: Got him, O'Connor?

O'CONNOR: Yeah. Send for the wagon.

OFFICER: We got the car outside.

O'CONNOR [*sharply*]: Send for the wagon!

OFFICER: Okay. [*He goes to the phone.*]

GLORY [*in a breathless whisper*]: Terry—you ain't hurt bad?

TERRY [*tiredly as he leans against wall*]: Naw, they just winged me, that's all.

GLORY: I tried to stop 'em, Terry—I tried as hard as I could!

TERRY [*panting*]: I know. It's all right. [*To O'Connor:*] Let go of the girl. You ain't got nothing on her. She don't know who I am, even.

O'CONNOR: Naw?

TERRY: Let her come here for a minute. Go on. It won't hurt nothing.

GLORY: Yes! Please!

O'CONNOR: All right, sister. [*He releases her. She falls, sobbing beside Terry on the bench.*]

TERRY: What's the difference to you? You'll be the same as you was before I come to this place. Only you'll be better off.

GLORY: Terry, Terry!

TERRY: Gimme a cigarette, will you?

O'CONNOR: Wagon coming?

OFFICER: On the way.

TERRY: I'm not your kind. Me an' you, we couldn't have gone on together. I wouldn't have stuck. I never stuck at anything, Macushla.* I was always running away. And now I still am— If

---

* Macushla— Irish for darling.

145

you coppers wanted to keep me locked up somewhere you should-n't have shot so goddamn many holes in my carcass for me to be running out through! [*He laughs.*] Hell, you can take my picture now an' hang it up in every post office from here to the rockbound coast of the moon—for all the good it'll ever do you! Glory . . . . [*The cigarette slips from his fingers.*]

[*The transients come slowly downstairs, singly, their dully curi-ous faces and shambling figures grotesquely lighted by the red bulb at the landing. They group themselves in a mumbling half-circle about the central figures of Terry, Glory and the offi-cers. Leo, wakened and sobered by what has happened, push-es through the men and goes to Glory's side. A police siren rises from the distance.*]

GLORY: Terry—I'm going *with* you, Terry!

OFFICER: If you do sister, you'll have to go a hell of a lot fur-ther'n the Laclede Avenue Police Station.

LEO: He's— ?

O'CONNOR: Gone.

[*The siren stops as the wagon draws up outside. The men lift Terry from the bench and carry him outside.*]

O'CONNOR: You men go back up to your beds.

[*They obey, mumbling among themselves, and looking curi-ously back.*]

O'CONNOR [*to Leo*]: Your sister, ain't she?

LEO: Yes.

O'CONNOR: I'll leave her with you.

[*He goes out. The room is left empty except for Leo and Glory. She sobs frenziedly on floor beside the bench. Leo moves to the window through which can be seen dimly the lights of the patrol wagon. The siren sounds again and fades as the wagon moves off.*]

GLORY [*wildly*]: They're taking him off!

LEO [*his voice is strong and clear*]: Not *him*. They never *caught* him. He said that he was still running away—and that's true . . .

[*The sky behind the city's towers brightens faintly during this speech. Snow can be seen falling through the arc light.*]

LEO: They'll never catch his kind till they learn that justice doesn't come out of gun barrels. —They'll never catch *us* either— Not till they tear down all the rotten old walls that they wanted to lock us up in! [*More quietly.*] Look, Glory. The snow's still falling. I guess that God's still asleep. [*Rising inflection.*] But in the morning maybe he'll wake up and see disaster! He'll hear the small boys' voices shouting the morning's news—"The Criminal's Captured, the Fugitive Returned!"—And maybe he'll be terribly angry at what they've done in his absence, these righteous fools that played at being God tonight and all the other nights while he's been sleeping! — [*Softly but with strong feeling.*] Or if he never wakes up—then we can play God, too, and face them out with courage and our own knowledge of right, and see whose masquerade turns out best in the end, theirs or ours— [*He slowly turns away from the window. Then, putting his arm around Glory.*] But tonight there's nothing left to be done but sleep for a time and forget, while the snow keeps on falling . . . .

CURTAINS CLOSE SLOWLY